The Transformation of Anna

Cornerstone Deep Book 1

The Transformation of Anna
Copyright © 2013 Charlene A. Wilson

Published by
Arched Spectrum Publishing
PO Box 1032
Morrilton, Arkansas 72110

Names, characters and incidents depicted in this book are products of the author's imagination or are used fictitiously. Any resemblance to actual events, locales, organizations, or persons, living or dead, is entirely coincidental and beyond the intent of the author or the publisher.

No part of this book may be reproduced or transmitted in any form or by any means, electronic or mechanical, including photocopying, recording, or by any information storage and retrieval system, without permission in writing from the publisher.

Credits
Cover Artist: Jennifer Brown
Editor: Susan Davis

ISBN-13: 978-0-9899846-0-7
ISBN-10: 0989984605

Printed in the United States of America

What People Are Saying

This is lyrical, beautiful, and poignant. It's such a fairytale and yet a paranormal romance! How she is able to ride that line is amazing.

— Nova
My Seryniti

Love knows no bounds and knows no space and the story of Anna and Cole is one incredible story.

— Kaiden's Seductions

Cornerstone Deep was a more than just a great read it was a fantastic, magical read.

— The Avid Reader

The love story compares only to say Romeo and Juliet or even The Princess Bride. It's real, true love and Charlene shows it with such wonderful emotion. It's beautiful!

— Anastasia V. Pergakis
Author of The Kinir Elite Chronicles

This is a romance with magical elements you won't want to miss.

— Kristine
A Bibliophile's Thoughts on Books

Dedication

For my mother
whose patience and quiet example of persistence
inspires me to never give up.

The Transformation of Anna

Cornerstone Deep Book 1

by
Charlene A. Wilson

Chapter One

Cole moved as smoke, his elements converted into a dark mass. The sweet aroma along the hillside orchards of Shilo Manor gave way to the pungent odor of east side sewage facilities. Though his speed made the encounter brief, he scoffed. *How this dimension has changed over the last eight hundred years.*

Pedestrians on Beggars Row East rushed from one shop to another, dodging the homeless who cluttered the walkway with their bundles. An engine groaned as a public bus rounded the corner and then paused, sending exhaust to wash along his essence. His scowl deepened to a glower at the nauseating fumes. *And the twentieth century seems to be the worst.*

He jetted through an alley and emerged into a compacted neighborhood. Faded paint colored the row of town houses. Tiny lawns sported more ruts and dirt than foliage. Children hopped from oil-stained curbs to asphalt as they played along the roadside. Fringe from the holes in their trousers flapped with each bound. Knitted caps tossed aside, the chill manifested in their cheerful cheeks.

Cole, an undulating vapor, paused beside a copse of honeysuckle. In a billow, he reclaimed his elements to solid form and plucked a few of the blossomed twigs. How perfect to find Charlotte's favorite flowers so near to their tryst—just the right addition for this special night. He stepped from the seclusion and then grimaced as he scanned the area. Weathered thresholds lined the motel cul-de-sac and bore dark smudges where someone scrubbed at obscene vandalism. Chunks of siding, broken or missing, left a snaggle-toothed appearance along the eaves. Cement walkways lining the structure crumbled at the curbs, worn down to join with the gravel lot. He pulled Charlotte's note from his vest pocket, double-checked the address, and then lifted his gaze to the flickering sign.

Hightower Nights.

Correct location. His heavy sigh misted in the spring air. *I told her to spare no expense and she chose this? No wonder the invoice was so low.*

Cole draped his overcoat on his arm. *We will attend the next ball the noblemen announce whether she likes it or not.*

He ran his palm over his scalp, smoothing his long hair, and then crossed the parking lot to the sidewalk. Tarnished room numbers led his way.

Thirty-three, thirty-two...

A door slammed. As he glanced in the direction, a dark head of curls hit his chest. Long ringlets bounced around her heart-shaped face as the young woman stumbled backward.

He grasped her arm so she wouldn't tumble off the failing curb. "Forgive me. I should have been watching my steps."

She caught her breath and smiled at him with dark brown eyes. "Oh, my fault, really. I'm running late and…" her thick lips teetered. "Um," she scanned him from head to foot.

Her emotions flew through him with a resounding *wow*, neighbored by the flush of her nerves and a distinct sense of envy. At times like these, he could do without the ability to perceive other people's feelings. She couldn't be much older than eighteen and to know what a child felt when she looked at him was uncomfortable to say the least.

Cole glanced at his tailored black vest and trousers. No doubt he was a conspicuous sight, given their surroundings. His snowy white sleeves alone declared he didn't belong among the stained and faded. His gaze caught her attention from her more than thorough perusal.

Her caramel complexion flushed. "Wow. Even your shoes are polished like glass. You've got to be Tom."

The comment caught him off guard and he flinched. Few knew his alias much less his real name. "Excuse me? Have we met?"

"I'm Amy." She giggled and motioned down the way. "Charlotte's my mother. She told me all about you. I thought she was exaggerating but," she bit her lip and her gaze flew over him once again. "It's so nice to meet you. I think it's great Mother's dating again. Oh, and I think it's so romantic you have a special way of saying her name."

Cole furled his brow.

Amy nodded. "Yeah, she told me all about it. *Sh'létte*. She says it makes her melt." Her nose wrinkled to meet the tight arch of her eyes and he thought she was going to giggle again. "You make my mother melt."

He stifled a groan at the comment.

Her eyes flitted to the honeysuckle he held. "Oh, you gathered her flowers, too. You know she loves honeysuckle. You are so sweet."

Her hand flew to his arm and he started. She suddenly displayed a serious expression. "And don't worry about the age difference thing. She said you were more my age but you act like a true gentleman." Amy nodded enthusiastically and her curls bounced around her head. "Yeah, she told me everything. She's worried it worries you. The age thing, that is. She's afraid you might think she's too old to, you know, have any more children. Since you don't have any of your own."

She rolled her eyes and blushed. "But she's not. And I'd love to have a little brother or sister. I'd baby-sit anytime you two wanted to—well you know—have private time."

Cole cleared his throat.

Amy leaned close. "She really, really likes you, Tom. She finally admitted it to me. But I've known for months. She even bought a new dress to wear tonight."

She held her hand up, palm facing him as if to stop him from what...listening? "Well, I bought her the dress. I just got paid. She's worried the style is too young for her, but I insisted ivory eyelets just aren't what women my age wear. It is nineteen-seventy-four after all. It's beautiful on her, really." She winked. "So you might mention it. Of course, as gentlemanly as you are, you'd probably mention it anyway." This time she giggled and Cole smiled, realizing Amy's genuine concern for her mother.

"I'll be sure to notice."

She shrugged her shoulders and squealed. "Mother is so lucky. The way you two look tonight you should be in a horse-drawn carriage going to a ball." She sighed. "Well, I'd love to stay and chat but I only took a break to run and get her some champagne. She wants tonight to be special." She waved a hyper hand. "I have to get back to work."

Turning to leave, she called to a woman across the lot. "Oh, Megan, grab that bus! Hey, you'll never guess who the new mail clerk is…"

Cole watched her bound to the woman. The girl definitely had her mother's free-flowing spirit. Still, the topics covered left a twinge in his cheek. He straightened to regain any dignity he'd lost through the discourse and continued down the path.

The number twenty-nine hung with the nine threatening to become a six. As he slid the key in the lock, it jammed half way home. Unwilling to wrestle the rusty thing, he waved his finger to the right and it released with a *clunk*.

He peered inside and found his date sitting on the floor. "Do I have the right place? I had to double-check the address."

Charlotte looked up from her seat in front of the imitation fireplace. Her dark curls cascaded down her back, leaving her tan shoulders bare. Tiny buttons ran up the bodice of her ivory dress. It hugged her while the gathered skirt flaunted layers of light ruffles that emphasized her feminine nature. Pulled up to her lap, her knees peeked from the hemline.

Amy was right, a beautiful choice, perfect for a ball and an embellished horse-drawn carriage.

She held out her hand. "Come sit with me."

He tossed his coat on the bed and sat behind her. As he wrapped her in his embrace, he couldn't resist pressing his lips to her collar.

"Mmm, you feel good," she hummed.

He presented the honeysuckle and as she smelled them, he had to ask. "What are you doing on the floor?"

"I'm watching the fire." She glanced over her shoulder, brown eyes twinkling. "I've always wanted to stay here. The fireplace makes it romantic."

Cole looked at the rolling screen of flames. Faux bricks of the hearth curled at the corner for lack of adhesive and the cardboard mantel dipped where someone sat a heavy object on the visual setting. A tiny *creak* sounded each time the rotating fireplace screen made a slow round.

"I see. Yes, fires are romantic." Shifting his gaze back to his reason for being there, he nuzzled her ear. "Is this a new gown?"

Her smile crinkled her eyes and she cuddled closer against him. "Do you like it?"

"It's lovely." He leaned his head to her dark curls. "Did you have me in mind when you picked it out?"

Her cheeks flushed as an answer.

"Definitely a romantic evening."

The joy of holding her, having her heart touch his, coursed through him as none had in decades...in centuries. He yearned to hear her soul speak to him. He widened his perception to read her tender emotions and brushed his lips along her shoulder. A hint of cotton candy met them when he reached the hollow beneath her ear. He smiled against her skin.

Flavored body spray? A youthful notion, no doubt encouraged by Amy. Pleasure rode his breath.

Combing her fingers through his long hair, she held him there. Her heated whisper fell to his palm as he reached to caress her cheek. "I love that. I love your lips on me."

Her words spurred his wish. "Talk to me, Sh'létte. Share everything with me. I want to know."

"The way you feel, Tom." She splayed her fingers over his head, holding him tighter. Her want echoed through his nerves and he sucked a breath as his teeth raked down her neck.

"The way you—move...all of it," she exclaimed.

The tiny buttons down her bodice popped from their eyelets as he released them one by one. Easing her back against the carpet, his lips caressed the soft skin of her cleavage. "I find joy in you. I want to hear from every part of you. Tonight, I want all of you."

"I want you too, Tom. My heart..."

A rumble sounded in his throat as he led his kisses to the heavy beat in her chest. "You're heart what?"

She cried with delectation.

Cole lifted his gaze. "Look at me."

Her lids fluttered open and her mouth moved with quiet breath. "I love you."

Pure acceptance radiated from her and he knew she did. But he needed to know this relationship would be more than those he'd ended in the past. He pinched his lips together. Gazing deeply into her wide irises, he focused intently to hear her response.

"*Open to me, Sh'létte,*" he whispered, sending his thought's voice with his words. "*Speak to me with your soul.*"

Her lips parted and astonishment flashed in her brown eyes. "Did I just hear you—in my head?"

He listened eagerly as her feelings poured through him in waves of confusion, adoration, thrill... Her gaze darted around his face, brows curling into question.

His heart sank. *Please don't be silent.* His voice came forth as a plea, but he didn't care. If only her soul would offer some form of communication. "Call to me, Sh'létte. I don't want this to end."

Her eyes flew wide. "What? End. No, Tom, what do you mean? You have my whole heart. I couldn't be more open to you—ever." She curled her fingers in his hair. "What is it? Is there something you worry about in our relationship? Is it my age? Are you worried I can't give you a family? It's not too late for me. I'd love to give you a child. I'm as open as I can possibly be to you."

An ache wedged deep within his chest. Her emotions flowed inside him like a tidal wave. Surely, her soul would speak soon.

"Oh, my love. Let me help you," he whispered. With final hope, he called upon his foreign nature to share the most seductive gift of his home realm. The scent of licorice and cream fell from his lips as he released the sweet Breath of Zephyr. He kissed her gently, caressed her tongue with his and sent his entreaty to bathe her senses. His breath became hers.

She inhaled and gasped as if she couldn't quench her thirst. Her love coursed through his veins, his muscles tightened with expectation.

"*Call to me!*" he bade with shared thought.

Her head pressed into the worn carpet as the sensation overpowered her. He framed her face to keep the connection, every fiber of his being watching for a sign. His heart rammed against his ribs, anticipation sizzled down his spine. "*Please. Call to me.*"

A hum rose in Charlotte's throat and as she released her breath, her hands slid down his arms. Cole peered into her hooded eyes as she drunkenly looked up at him. "Oh, Gods, Tom. I love you."

Fact lodged reality into Coles mind, forcing him

to see the truth. Tiny tremors rode his muscles. His lips teetered into a smile to hide his disappointment. A true soul mate would have responded to such a call.

Their relationship was only a passing moment in his very long life. The knowledge bit at his heart. Leaning on his elbow, he traced the heart-shaped curve of her face from cheek to chin with his fingertips.

This would have to be their last night together.

The morning chill followed Cole through the cherry-wood door of Shilo Manor. Apricot blossoms rode the breeze and danced across the hardwood floor. His brothers' attention drew away from their conversation beside the marble staircase sentinel to his homecoming.

James smiled, his dimpled cheeks forcing his eyes to grin. "How's Charlotte? I trust things went well."

Cole glanced at him as he hung his coat on the gold rack. "Yeah," his voice fell flat.

Vincent set his hands at his waist and his chiseled features leered. "Don't tell me. You dumped another one."

James held up his large hand to halt further comment. His smile faded.

With a heavy step, Cole crossed the hall to the parlor and glowered at the smiling cherubim that lined the wall. From the doorway he glanced at his youngest brother shaking his unruly hair.

Vincent settled and glared at Cole. "I had real

hopes for this one. You've seen her longer than any of the others. It's been what? A whole four months?"

Cole turned, entered the parlor, and slammed the door behind him.

Irritating runt.

He stepped to the cherry-wood bar and stared at the wide variety. An entire wall displayed the finest liqueur this realm had to offer along with a few choice Ambrosias brought from theirs' to this post. He consciously avoided the ancient keeps, unwilling to recall the joy of that era.

He smoothed his long hair with his hands and grabbed the nearest bottle. Brown liquid filled his glass to the brim. He downed half the bitter take before a tap came from the door. James entered and closed it quietly. "Don't mind Vince."

Resentment filled Cole's throat like bile and he was sure his expression displayed it.

His brother sighed and looked out over the room.

"I wanted this woman more than any since..." He frowned and slugged his drink. "Her soul was silent." He didn't bother hiding the disillusionment in his tone. "I couldn't reach her."

"Don't do this to yourself, Cole. You can't expect another Mianna."

"I can't settle for less than a soul mate, James. Not now."

"The fact that you found a soul mate in her is phenomenal. But she's gone. Rebirth doesn't exist here. You have to let her go and move on." He looked at him with compassion. "Let yourself love Charlotte for who she is."

Cole lowered his glass to the bar and closed his eyes. The sting of reality pierced his heart. "I can't,

James." He looked at his brother and swallowed hard. "I try. But my soul always pushes for more."

James lowered his gaze and his voice softened. "You know cross dimension mating is limited. Chances are you're not going to find that kind of connection again. Not here."

He turned away, knowing it was foolish to allow himself the hope for that kind of love with Charlotte. Mianna had been special.

Chapter Two

Anna's vision hazed and her concentration waned. *What an order.* This job was the most demanding she'd been assigned; one that held consequences she'd rather avoid if not completed to the bidder's taste.

She slid off her stool and stretched her back, scanning the colorful shapes on the work table. It filled much of her art studio, sitting at the center for easy access to all sides. The island held two completed zinc-bonded works. Another three-by-five foot panel lay nearly finished over the pattern of palm-sized sketches.

She swept the shard and metal bits into the trash bin and dragged her wrist across her brow. Grabbing her coffee mug, she sighed and dumped the cold remains down the corner sink. "Three more panels."

The department assistant peeked around the door frame. "Hey, Anna."

Her cheerful voice grated on Anna's fatigued nerves and she cringed. "Hi, Amy."

"I noticed you were still working when I left last night. I know this is a big assignment, but be careful. You're pushing it with the new curfew."

"I have a deadline. I can't afford to lose my job over this."

"Well, my mother dates a guy that's," she formed quotes with her fingers, "in-the-know, and he told her to take it very seriously."

Steam rose as Anna poured a fresh cup of coffee from the percolator. Vanilla cream sweetened the mix to her taste. "I heard the announcement. And I'm sure they exaggerated a bit."

Amy shook her head. "He said anyone out past curfew that was alive and breathing could be targeted and never heard from again." She nodded and her dark curls bounced around her shoulders. "Yeah, he said it was serious. And I believe him. I met him, and he really looks like he's in-the-know. Not just an announcer type. So be careful."

Anna lifted the corners of her mouth into a forced smile. "Okay. Thanks."

"Well, just thought I'd remind you." She shuffled the bundles of mail to her other arm and pranced out the door. Her cheery greeting sang down the hall from the next studio.

Anna sipped at the drink as she turned to her creation. The glass artwork sparkled beneath the fluorescent studio lights. As required, not one design that made up the trio was identical. The stained-glass montage blurred into abstraction and she pressed her thumb and fingers to her temples.

"This is impossible." Her cup teetered on a wipe-rag as she sat it down and then pulled her dark hair back into a ponytail.

"That's why I chose you for the job."

Startled, she turned toward the deep voice. Lord Dressen's lips curled into a crooked smile. He tucked his hand under his tailored overcoat and rested it in his pants pocket. A gift box cradled in his other hand as he sauntered to her. "I know your work. And I know you won't disappoint."

She offered a small smile. She needed a break, but he was not that kind of break. "I'll do my best. But if you want me to finish on time, you really should stop dropping by. It only distracts me."

He furled his heavy brows. "I like that I distract you. Besides," he opened the box and set a bejeweled bowl on the table. "I brought you a gift, and I wanted to see those blue eyes sparkle when I gave it to you."

Anna glanced at the shallow treasure. Gems adorned the black lacquered surface and gleamed in the bright lights. *At least it's not another piece of jewelry.* As beautiful as they were, there would never be an occasion to wear them among her social class. She could at least use this for a…candy dish?

She mimicked a grateful acceptance.

He grinned and withdrew another item from his jacket's inner pocket. Removing the tissue wrap, he placed a thick black candle in the center of the holder.

"A candle. A black one." She upped her eyes and blinked. "It'll go nicely with my yellow wallpaper." Anna suppressed the urge to snigger.

His lips widened to a toothy grin. Withdrawing a silver box from his pocket, he pulled out a match and struck it against the side of the container. As the wick flamed to life, a sensual aroma of licorice and vanilla filled the air.

Her snigger melted to awe. Her cheeks warmed and her senses instantly lulled as tension fled. Her body relaxed, and Anna couldn't hold back her delight. Such a unique sensation. She breathed deep to let it filter through her body. Her soul drank in the tranquil essence like a forgotten addiction. A serene veil coated her mind, and she set a hand on the table to steady the effect.

"You like the gift."

She looked at him, afraid to admit it, but knew it showed on every inch of her.

Dressen nodded and brushed the art tools far to the side. "I chose this scent." He took her hand then backed her against the table. "Had it made for you."

His gray eyes looked into hers. "I can give you anything, Anna. Wealth, security, love. I could be the soul mate you want."

Anna's knees weakened and she gazed at him with wonder. How long had he pursued her? Longer than he should have, given she offered no welcome to his advances. A year? More? Gold, jewels, exotic flowers—they were all propositions during his persistent courtship. He'd even offered travels to the only thriving Arylin colony in existence. That was a hard one to refuse.

Unconnected memories gathered as the thick candle scent touched her. Her chest tightened with her heartbeat, and she raised her gaze to his. A longing for his touch, that before now seemed so ridiculous, pooled in her core. She allowed his hands to skim around her waist and hold her.

Placing her hand to his cheek, she traced the narrow features as if seeing them for the first time. Instead of aristocratic pomp, his face was kind. Patient.

Something filled her with what she'd always sought. Something familiar to her spirit, her soul. Why had she turned him down all this time? She brushed her fingers across his silvering hair. How could she have been so blind to him?

He cupped her hand with his. "Tell me, Anna. Tell me you want what I do." He stroked loose strands of her hair back and grasped the locks in her ponytail. "I won't wait much longer."

"Kyle, I..."

His eyes lighted and he smiled. "Say that again."

His words forced her to focus. "What?"

"My name. Say it again."

"Um," her mind stumbled, and she took a deep breath to clear her thoughts. *Did I just let myself be informal with a Nobleman?* "Lord Dressen, I don't...think this is a good idea." *Well, that wasn't very convincing.*

His dark gaze twinkled with a flash of victory. "You just called me Kyle. And I think this is a very good idea. You won't be disappointed."

He pulled her close as if her weak rebuttal was an open invitation. His hot breath bathed her lips. "I've wanted you so long. Tell me you want me, too."

He didn't wait for an answer. His lips crushed against hers in a hungry kiss.

Anna gasped. *Wait! What have I done to bring this on? Nothing. I've done nothing!* Wedging her elbows against his chest, she shoved. A low growl rumbled in his throat.

Fear rushed from her gut to her cheeks as he pinned her against the table and pressed her to recline.

Dear Arylin, Goddess of Love, help me!

"Oh, um, excuse me."

Amy's perky voice came from the door, and Lord Dressen shot a scowl over his shoulder. He straightened and slid his hands from Anna.

She inched past him and closed the gap between them with quick strides. "Amy, hi!"

Amy glanced at Dressen and bit her lip. "I'm sorry to interrupt, Anna. But Mr. Cantrell wanted me to get this to you. Specifications on the revised order."

She received the envelope with a shaky hand and pulled out the plans. "Revised order?"

Dressen grinned.

"You changed your order with Mr. Cantrell? A circle of fused glass at the center of each?" She looked at him bewildered. "Three are nearly completed already. Do you realize the extra time this will take?"

"I need them by the thirteenth." He strolled to her. "Mr. Cantrell understands the gravity of my satisfaction. I'm sure you don't want to compromise the standing of Cantrell Artisan. It would be devastating to the company." He stepped between the two and whispered into her ear. "Of course, none of this would matter if you'd just say—yes." He cocked a grin and winked, sauntering out of the room.

Amy giggled beneath her fingers. "Anna, I can't believe you aren't with him already. Everyone knows he wants you. We're all so envious!" She glanced at the table. "And it looked like you two are...well..." she giggled again. "Why don't you just agree? It's not like you have anything holding you back. That rutty row house? The stove and heating never work properly. You're so far behind in the bills you're about to lose it anyway. Especially after you had to fix all the vandalism to the property. Honestly, that neighborhood reeks." She leaned her head to Anna. "No offense."

Anna's stomach churned.

"You'd have a big Chalice Wedding. You'd become a Lady and live in that mansion with all those servants. Sure, he's older but he's not that bad looking. Mother's dating a much younger guy. Really, age is nothing these days. Anna, he's a Grand Marshal!" She leaned her head in a sweet gesture. "And if your father was still alive, it'd make him so proud. He loved you so much and worked so hard to raise you alone. A street sweep's daughter becoming a Lady. It really would make him proud."

Anna let her hands fall to her side and glanced to where the unexpected kiss had taken place. What a dirty shot, bringing her father into this. She closed her eyes at his memory.

"Amy," she whispered. "Never use my father like that again."

The mantle clock chimed and Cole looked at the old timepiece. He glowered as the throaty tone sounded and then fell silent. If it wasn't a priceless treasure, he'd crush the wretched thing. For centuries, the deep tone sang of how slowly time passed...as if he needed reminding another empty hour had gone by without her.

He glided his thumb down the smooth side of the family's Candle Vignette. The enchanted record keeper fit perfectly in his palm, nested by his fingers. For the life of him, he couldn't remember never loving the relic.

His gaze shifted to the amber glow that emitted from the cleft in the top. It framed a picture of the past with a faded margin. The image undulated with gentle waves, the subject's heartbeat influencing the life of the memory. Love touched his senses with every pulse. Blue eyes twinkled at him and bow-tie lips curved upward in a natural smile against the cherubic face. Her long dark ringlets rested on her petite shoulders, the same locks that would surround him with the scent of roses when he had relished the soft skin at her neck.

Four hundred years. Cole swallowed the tightness in his throat and let a breath speak her name. "Mianna."

Footsteps came from the hall, and James leaned his head inside the doorway. "I thought I'd find you here."

He pursed his lips and waved a hand over the picture album. The depiction faded. "Meaning?"

"Whenever you've courted a woman as long as you have this time, you retreat to the study."

Probably true, it seemed to be the only place he found solace. The tapestries hanging along the east wall were the closest thing to home with the blue sun of Meridian and the moons that cast an indigo glow. It seemed to soothe him somewhat.

He longed for the gifted dimension. Yet he searched for love here, in Cornerstone Deep—for the soul who had touched his so long ago.

Cole sighed. "Did you need something?"

James eased into the seat beside him and laced his thick fingers over his waist. "We found a harvest subject for Lord Dressen's order."

Vincent stepped in and leaned on the door frame, his squared jaw set in silence.

Cole looked back at the Vignette. "The spell's ready. Are you sure she fits all the requirements?"

With a nod, James glanced at Vincent who looked away. Strong emotions touched Cole's senses as his brothers' feelings rolled off them in hot waves;

uncertainty, distaste, skepticism... And he didn't blame them. This bid was definitely out of the ordinary, as was the new decree.

"Curfew breaker?"

James nodded again.

"Okay." Cole set the instrument on the desk and smoothed back his hair. "Details."

James passed a finger over his wristwatch. The luminescent face throbbed blue. "Age, twenty-five. Approximate height, five feet five inches. Light complexion, dark hair. City's lower east side resident." He leaned forward and looked back at Cole. "She's acceptable for the position."

Cole stood and summoned his cloak. It flew through the door into his hand. "Name?"

"Anna Sinclair. She's been getting home moments late. Without the shortcut through Shilo Park she'll be out well past the allotted curfew."

"We won't find another to match such a bid." Cole slung the cape over his shoulders and secured the clasp. "Lock the north entrance."

Vincent's features matched the stony countenance of the statue beside him. Raising his hand, he pointed it toward town. Tiny sparks spangled across his knuckles as he snapped his fingers into a fist. He spoke through his teeth. "It's secure."

James raised his brow. "That's Gryffin's perch."

"Gryffin knows of the new law by now. His silence on the matter proves this is no different from any other duty we perform." Cole glanced at the wide tapestries that hung along the east wall of the study. *Meridian.* His home realm. Nostalgia gnawed at his stomach as did the reasons their God of Conformance remained silent. "And I gave up caring a long time ago."

He stepped back and grasped the edge of his cloak. On cue, his brothers furled their capes. A dark mist overtook them as they dispersed their elements into the Smoke of Night. Their essences darted from the study down the hall. The front door flew open and crisp spring air penetrated Cole's being. He led the way over the manor hedge and down the southern hillside to the City of Shilo.

Chapter Three

The lights died and shadows replaced the candescent glare. Anna threw her gaze to the window. Dusk.

She slid the aromatic candle closer, using the dim light to finish positioning the intricate glass forms. Its stout core had lessened over the hours she'd worked. Though she thought about snuffing out the gift after Dressen's actions, she couldn't bring herself to extinguish the comforting scent.

Cursed time. She draped her work station with a light cloth and threw on her jacket. With the bejeweled candleholder tight in her grip, she rushed out the door. The scent of licorice and vanilla trailed from the flame as she weaved her way through adjoining art studios and corridors.

As she emerged from Cantrell Artisan, she shivered in the spring air. Sulfuric odor from the industrial west side rode the breeze from across town and the fragrant fire flickered out. She cradled the holder between the large granite lion paws that sat beside the steps. It fit nicely. She sniggered at the sight.

Kyle Dressen's artistic contribution to the sphinx.

She stepped onto the sidewalk and looked around. Humor faded. Vapor loomed over the empty streets like phantoms gathering warmth from the asphalt. She briskly rubbed her sleeves. The slight warming did nothing to ease her insecurity. Street lights blinked on but offered little comfort as the newscaster's announcement flooded her mind.

"After much deliberation, the new curfew of 1974 has been set into place. Lord Kyle Dressen, Grand Marshal of the courts, announced the bill's passing, and urges all to adhere as strict measure will be taken to ensure vandalism of the east side is eradicated."

What a ridiculous notion, the impoverished east side getting aid from the lawmakers.

Yet now, unease filled her. Her co-workers' gossip on the matter didn't help her anxiety. An apprehensive tone caught her voice as she repeated the warning aloud, "Curfew breakers will never be seen again." Her whisper sent mist through the chill. She wished she hadn't spoken.

Anna hurried across the open court and down an adjacent street. Awnings rustled in the wind. Neon signs that once invited late-night commerce hung dead behind barred windows. Her rushed steps echoed through the air.

She looked to the sky. A blanket of stars covered the firmament. She'd worked too late. Again. "Gods, I'm not going to make it."

Her steps quickened and she caught her breath as she approached the shortcut through the park. The wide corner entrance stood closed. The ancient stone griffin perched high on the gateway glared down at her. She shook the bars with disbelief and scanned the long gates that fortified the urban green.

Fear clutched her stomach. "When do they ever lock Shilo Park?"

"Anna."

The voice whispered in her mind, clear as if spoken. She whipped around and studied the shadowed pavement. Beneath the dim light of a street lamp, dense smoke billowed, taking the form of three men. Her throat clenched.

"What...in...the...world!" She spun around and ran.

"There's no use in running."

Throwing her hands to her ears, she tried to block out the voice. An abandoned shuttle van propped halfway up the curb offered the only protection along the vacant street. She darted across the road to find refuge.

Her long hair netted over her face as she stumbled past street-side clutter. She swiped the strands away. Catching her balance, she raced along the storefronts and spotted a weak halo down an alley. *An open door?* She rushed into the darkness.

Puddles of discarded waste filled the dips in the pass and the air was thick with a foul stench. Her frantic feet beat the pavement as she raced to every locked door.

Steady footsteps followed.

She gasped with each failed entry. "Come on. Just one open door."

A cry ripped her throat as she turned to the final promise of safety. A small lamp flickered. Obscene graffiti sprawled the length of the wall that blocked her escape; a dim halo highlighted the neon paint.

She turned to the way she came and stared at the forms as they overtook the narrow alley. A man led center, his companions flanking. Each unified stride caused their capes to furl with controlled motion. The bleak lamp lit their approach—a dark trio. Reapers, all of them—black hair, black eyes, black cloaks. *Curfew breakers are never seen again.* At that moment, she believed.

Her body trembled and she backed into a corner for support. "This is a nightmare." Her shallow voice quivered and sent denial through her. "This isn't happening!" The tomb-like closure briefly echoed her claim but the measured steps resounded as they approached.

Anna held her breath as if to ward off the imminent danger. They stopped a few feet from her and the leader stepped forward.

Endless time filled her as she gazed at their resolute faces. She swallowed hard to ward off the want of air.

The leader lifted his hand as if setting a butterfly free. A mist, the brilliance of snow crystalline, encircled her and lingered in the air.

Anna struggled to withhold a gasp.

"You have to breathe sometime."

The voice sifted through her mind. Her lungs burned, begged for relief. Fear gripped her as she succumbed to need and the tiny crystallites flowed past her lips.

The taste of divinity touched her senses and the promise of bliss sang in her mind. The invitation was overwhelming, irresistible. A wave of serenity coated her emotions.

She met his gaze.

A small smile touched his coal eyes. It penetrated her soul. Opposition dissolved.

He inhaled the sparkling mist and leaned close. Cradling her face in his hands, he touched his lips to hers. They were warm and seductive, unexpectedly tender. The aroma of licorice and cream flowed through her. She accepted his attention, intoxicated by the offering. In a gentle motion, his tongue lovingly caressed hers. Eternity echoed in her heart.

With a breath, the magic spell filled her. Heat steamed her lungs and filtered throughout her body. Every wave carried with it memories; the last words of her father, the aged photo of her mother she clung to as a child.

Subjection engulfed her mind. All wonderment ceased under its capture. Rapture sealed her senses and final will vanished.

Anna weakened beneath Cole's touch. Her mouth relaxed, face stilled. He rose from the tender moment startled by his actions. They were entirely uncalled for, unexpected, yet he couldn't deny the pleasure it brought.

He stared at her as she wavered with the effects of empty thought. This girl had indeed sought refuge from her life's experiences. By her complete surrender, he had no doubt she'd wished for the chance to forget many times—a common occurrence among the homeless. He allowed the spell's sparkling enchantment to fade. No further need for it with this one. This harvest was complete.

As she opened her eyes, he gazed deeply into them to offer hope and set the desire to take pride in her service. *"Your life will find meaning."*

Her gaze wandered amongst them. James, his strong stature evident beneath his cloak, would intimidate many without the effects of the charm. Though distinction trimmed his features, she seemed to be taken by his dimple-kissed cheeks and brushed her own.

Vincent was next. Her head leaned a little as she studied him. Smaller in build, he still radiated strength. His deep onyx eyes held his defined brow low. Square jaw set, he looked as if vengeance ruled his core. His untamed locks fell in loose waves past his cheeks. A radiant glow encircled his clenched fists as they clutched his cape.

Cole watched as her gaze returned to him. His lips tightened together as his jaw tensed. She scanned his long hair as if to see how far it fell down his back.

When her gaze met his, he had to touch that angelic face. He raised his hand, but caught himself and straightened to his full height, squaring his shoulders. *What was that pull to touch?* It was unsettling. He clasped the edge of his cloak and turned.

Leading the way back down the alley, James and Vincent fell into step behind Cole. Anna gasped, then followed.

The litter from the empty street scurried from their path. Night birds sang from high on their perches, a melody odd in the darkness of the empty streets.

A vagabond sat beside the center fountain. Cole pulled Anna to him and wrapped an arm around her waist. He lifted his cloak with a furl and took on the Smoke of Night before the man could catch their approach.

Giggles and thrills flew through his senses as the young woman's emotions reacted to the disembodiment. He smiled to himself. Most accompanied him with calm acceptance. This girl seemed to embrace the experience.

As they reached the wide steps to the Grand Marshal's estate, Cole pulled at their elements to solidify. Anna held to him, her arms wrapped around his neck. Her warm breath puffed against his ear as he grabbed her waist so she wouldn't fall. *Was she holding me the whole time?*

He eased her down his chest until her toes touched the ground and arms left his shoulders. Running his palm down his shirt to regain his dignity, he strode past the border hedge onto the grounds. He glanced over his shoulder and she drew her hands to her bosom, innocence echoing from her heart.

Luminescent bobbles peaked from beneath bulbous shrubs, lighting the footpath with a radiant glow. Cole looked at the frontage of the imposing mansion. Three stories of white brick stretched out on both sides of a montage of stained glass that arched around the receiving hall doors. He'd never appreciated the over-indulgence of this Grand Marshal, known for his eccentric views and tastes. He seemed more eager to flaunt his position than most.

As they neared the gaudy threshold, he reached ahead and knocked twice with a heavy drive. The left panel opened and a lanky man peered out. His basset hound visage immediately woke at their presence.

"Good evening, sirs." The servant quickly stepped back and opened the door wide. "I'll fetch the sire."

"Yes."

Anna's gaze bore into Cole at the word. Heat flushed his cheeks and he stepped inside before his brothers noticed.

A screen of sparkling crystals adorned the left wall, neighbored by onyx pillars. To the right, a rash of brass hair lines cascaded the pane between two doors like a million squirming worms looking to invade the upper rooms. Sculptures of oversized silver swans stood at each side of the wide staircases, reflecting the multitude of embedded lights in the domed ceiling. Black veins in the white marble floor continued up the divided staircases leading to the enormous stained-glass window at the center of the back wall.

The sire's deep voice rang from the left wing hallway. Cole straightened as he neared.

"Sir Cole. It's good to see the three of you here." His gaze gravitated to Anna and a wash of satisfaction covered his face. "The addition, I see."

"As per your bid, she will comply completely. The harvest was a solid take." He looked back at the lawmaker. "I see she pleases you."

Dressen smiled and withdrew an envelope from his vest. "Oh, yes."

Holding up his hand, Cole shook his head. "I believe the fee is double for this one. Your requirements were very specific. Far beyond that of a Grand Marshal's standard order. So much so, a special spell was created to ensure satisfaction."

The sire chuckled and his smile tilted as he pocketed the payment. "Very well. I'll have the funds delivered in the morn. The Wizards of Shilo Manor continue to exceed their reputation. You are true Reapers."

The nickname wedged in Cole's gut. It screamed mockery to their position as Sentinels in this realm. Noblemen had always known they could manipulate the elements purely by their nature and advanced heritage. Yet this generation insisted on labeling them as a demon child at play. *Reapers. Wizards.* It knotted his stomach.

Intent on making the visit as short as possible, Cole turned his attention to Anna. *"Lord Dressen is now your keeper."*

Her regard shifted from him to the Grand Marshal and with it the adoration that had poured from her.

To Cole's surprise, he regretted the release to Dressen's care. Countless subjects had been harvested for service to the lords. The assignment of a keeper was an essential step. Why, then, would one more be any different? He reminded himself they had just completed another task, fully satisfying the order.

Dressen waved away the hound-faced servant and dismissed them himself. "Thank you, Sir Cole. It's rare to find such dedication to quality. You have never failed to produce astounding results." He grasped the handle and his gray eyes sparkled. "I must admit, I find your natures very compelling. Meridian must be an amazing dimension."

Underlying meaning seeped through Cole and he straightened to temper a scowl. "Thank you, Lord Dressen. We're pleased you find our work satisfactory."

Dressen shook his head. "Silent on the matter as ever." He chuckled. "Well, do watch for an invitation to my forthcoming celebration. I would be honored to have you present."

"Of course." Cole turned and crossed the threshold to avoid further remark. As the door closed behind them, Vincent's chiseled features contorted into rage.

Cole furled his cloak and took on the Smoke of Night before a confrontation could erupt. The last thing he needed was the runt's temperamental trantrums.

Vincent billowed like the crest of a storm as they flew over the dark city. His brothers' emotions melded to his; James' concern and confusion, and Vincent's pure fury. Small jets of lightning darted through their mass and Cole knew it was directed solely on him.

Chapter Four

Anna watched Lord Dressen as he closed the door. Reverence filled her. Every line that accented his heavy brow and creased his narrow face declared his wisdom. His dark hair was as a crown tinted with silver.

"Clair." His deep voice vibrated in her senses and touched her like warm honey. A woman appeared from the hall. "Anna has joined the household. She will fill the special bid and have the room on the second floor. See to it she knows what's expected of her."

"Yes, sire."

As he turned, his gaze lingered with a cocked grin. A low chuckle rode his breath and he disappeared down the hall.

Confusion entered as Anna's keeper departed. She darted her gaze around the spacious room. Lustrous onyx, polished silver and a brilliant ceiling commanded her view. The many eccentricities in the foyer sent anxiety raging and she searched for her tall savior for reprieve. He was gone. Panic flew.

Clair placed her hand on Anna's arm. "Come with me, love."

Anna watched her as she led the way. The woman's brown hair was tied back into a bun and her ferrety features wore a tiny smile. Small comfort settled the sting of desertion.

Marble staircases curved beside a masterful stained-glass window standing center stage on the far wall. Anna stared at the work of art that took up space from floor to vaulted ceiling. The geometric shapes absorbed her attention but her escort tugged her hand.

"You'll be staying on the second floor." They entered a long corridor and the servant opened the first door on the right.

"This is your room. Lord Dressen's is the master suite down the hall." She crossed the plush carpet to a set of glass doors and opened them. "The fresh air will help you relax. I know this is confusing to you." She turned on the light in a small hall to the right. "But really, the choice of lost memory is a blessing. There are twenty of us serving here under Lord Dressen and not a one regrets it. Some have been here since he gained his Lordship. Oh, I guess that'd be about forty years gone now. Reg, the butler was one of his originals. Nice man, Reg."

Clair slid the closet doors aside and removed a blue lounging robe. She peeked at Anna through her lashes as she handed it to her. "So, tell me. We're all so curious. How does it feel?"

Anna blinked at the woman. "How does it feel?"

She nodded with a little snigger. "We were told his order had strict requirements this time. You're a special one, you are, if you fit the bill. We hear you're to be on his arm."

"On his arm?"

The woman's brow furled. "Well," she closed the closet. "Maybe we can talk later when you've settled in. Just get bathed and dress for bed. I'll be back when you're done. There are a few things you need to know."

Panic flashed as the woman headed for the door. She grasped at the gown and rushed to her side. "You'll be back when I'm done?"

"You just get cleaned up and ready for bed. And welcome home."

The door closed behind her. Finality. Abandoned...again. Anna looked over her shoulder, scanning the room with apprehension. A burgundy comforter hugged the wide bed at the center of the far wall. A desk and chest of drawers took up the left. Stained-glass lampshades with matching light posts adorned the bed stands and a sculpture of a human form stood in the far right corner.

Fear held Anna's gaze as her vision widened to take in the scene as a whole. The items seemed to leer. In a shift of understanding, they morphed into rudimentary shapes and flattened against the wallpaper backdrop.

Alarm rang in her heart, pumping ice through her arms and legs. She darted into the little hall and entered the small room, slamming the door behind her. Heaving air, she turned to find a broad sunken bathtub, a toilet, and an oval sink.

She rushed to the tub and spun the water knob on. A wide stream gushed from a hole in the wall and down an angled ledge. Stripping off her clothes, she slipped in and sat. Droplets nettled her legs with each splash, pushing the anxiety further. She pulled her knees to her chest.

"She'll be back when I'm done." The words reassured her.

She sloshed her feet at the water as impatience mounted. A scowl scrunched her face and she turned off the flow. Snatching the soap, she slid it over her hair, across her shoulder, and then down between her breasts to her tummy. A large plop sounded at her feet as she threw it aside and dipped under the water to rinse. Done.

Trailing water across the rose tiled floor, she grabbed the gown and slipped it over her head. It clung to her wet skin as she pulled it down her torso. She tossed her hair over her shoulders.

Darting for the bedroom, motion in her periphery caught her attention. She halted at the door and looked back around the frame.

A woman.

Angst melted and she stepped back into the short hall, pulled the bench from under the counter, and sat. Adornments, perfumes, lotions, and puffs lined the narrow shelf. Seated on the other side, the lady's big blue eyes stared at her. Her angelic face was flushed red, long dark hair straggled and wet. The nightdress she wore stuck to her body as if drenched by rain, but the woman didn't appear to care.

Anna smiled at her and she returned the gesture. She waited to see what the woman would say. Silence.

"It's okay," Anna whispered. "I'll wait until you want to talk."

Cole planned to materialize on the porch first, but as it turned out, his brothers seemed to have the same goal.

James held his hand at Vincent's chest, allowing Cole to enter the manor first. The receiving hall welcomed him home with cherubim-laced walls and trim. But his irritated steps struck the hardwood floor with reverberant thuds as he pulled at the clasp of his cape. He tossed it, draping a sentinel beside the banister. It landed on the seraphim's head. He scowled and flicked his wrist, sending it from the statue to the coat rack.

James hung his cloak beside it.

Cole turned to face them as Vincent sent a bolt of energy to slam the door. The tall decorative windows on each side of the entrance burst and crashed to the floor. The cascading chandelier shook above them.

He glowered at the childish display. "I filled his order."

Vincent flung his cape to the floor. "You bound her soul!"

James waved at the shattered entrance. Shard and spar whirled into the air, each reclaiming its former place with tiny *clinks*.

Cole's heart hardened at the charge and he headed to the parlor. *Bound her soul.* "It was the only way to ensure complete compliance." A weak defense, he knew, but the only one that came to mind. He scanned the ample selection of liqueur that filled the wall. "She'll be happier than anyone in that house."

"Only because she won't know better not to." Vincent widened his stand with a step. "Sealing that spell with a kiss pushed the limit, Cole. You went too far this time!"

"We've been pushing the limit for centuries." With a swagger, he picked out a flask. "Now just get this all out of your system so we can get on with our lives. James is here to clean up your mess."

Vincent growled and a blue pulse jetted across the room from his fist, bursting the bottom of the bottle.

Cole pursed his lips and looked at him. He pointedly set the emptied selection on the bar and brushed the front of his shirt.

James bit back a grin.

He opened the cooler and chose a can of beer instead. "Okay, Kid. You want my attention." Popping open the drink, he faced Vincent and waved a dismissive hand. "Say what you have to say and be done."

"Her soul! Cole, how can you be so casual about this?"

"I told you. There was no other way to ensure complete compliance." He took a lengthy drink. "That man's order was impossible."

"You strengthened the spell. It would have brought her close enough."

"Close isn't good enough. We deliver what's ordered."

Vincent shook his head. "Father would have never approved of this. You know that!"

He scowled at the choice of weapon.

His youngest brother set his jaw with their father's memory backing every word. "He only agreed to gather the homeless to ensure their security, give them shelter. The Grand Marshals do that."

Cole slugged the remainder of his drink to drown the want to lash out. He slammed the empty can on the bar. "Giving them shelter." He scoffed. "Right along with memory wiping and bending wills."

Vincent turned livid. "That was only to appease the lords. It was to help the insecure settle. No real harm comes from that. Father loved these people!"

"And they're the very ones who ended him aren't they?" Cole sent his disgruntlement to the room. The leather seating and cherry fitments stood firm and offered his case no support. The picture window revealed the black night of this world—a cruel reinforcement that their assignment here was an indefinite curse to him. He threw his hand across the scene. The draperies whipped closed.

He set his clenched fist on the bar. "We did our job. The new law made her no different from any of the others we harvest." His voice lowered to a mumble. "What's binding a soul to a soul with no rebirth?"

His gaze flicked to the large masterpiece above the hearth. His father's dark eyes peered down at him and a flash of reproach stung his soul. He looked away to erase the discomfort.

James sat in a nearby chair and blew a long stream of air through his pursed lips. "I was going to wait until later for all of this, but I have to chime in here."

Furling his brow, Cole held up his can in a salute. "By all means, say your piece. At least I know you won't be spilling my drink all over my clothes."

James leaned his hulky arms on his knees. "I know how you feel about our situation, Cole. But we can't let bitterness shadow our reason for being in Cornerstone Deep. I don't believe Father would wish any ill on these people. Erasing memories allows the subjects to release the pain of their past. And bending wills enhances dedicated service, gives them a future to focus on. But a soul is a being's depth. Even if this dimension doesn't offer reincarnation it limits them to rely on the basic instincts of their nature."

Cole heaved a sigh. "All she'll know is that she's loved and wanted. You saw it in her eyes. Her whole heart was content at the thought of just being with us."

James shook his head. "At being with you. In her limited mind, you gave her life."

He paused at his brother's words and rolled his shoulder as discomfort struck his nerves. He swigged at his drink then calmed his voice. "When I turned her over to Lord Dressen, that reverence was given to him. Any attention he gives her will be like heaven to her. All mortals should be so lucky."

James held out his hand. "What's going to happen when she's left alone? Without a soul to guide her thoughts, emotions will take over. Confusion will lead to panic." He furrowed his brow. "Did any of this even enter your mind when you decided to seal that spell with a kiss?"

Cole growled. "I filled the man's order. What's done is done. If things go awry, I'll unbind the soul and refund the money."

A scowl accentuated Vincent's features. "That's it? You'll just undo everything and give back his money?"

James shook his head with a look of disbelief. "Have you ever unbound a soul, Cole? In nearly eight hundred years, have we *ever* unbound a soul?"

Sparks danced along Vincent's fisted fingers and he spoke through clinched teeth. "We've never *bound* a soul."

James glanced at the youngest and stood, stepping between the two. "Exactly. She's experiencing bliss right now. If you perform an unbinding—if it can be done at all—she'll regain her life's pain. She'll be in excruciating pain, Cole. We don't even know if she'd survive."

"I thought you were going to stay out of this."

James folded his arms across his broad chest and lifted his chin. "That was before you decided to play God."

Cole held up his hand and lowered his head in a small gesture of retreat. "Okay. The deed is done. I will personally keep posts on this girl and step in when needed." He slugged the remainder of his beer and set the can on the bar with a heavy fist. "But, trust me on this. There's not a more content woman in the world."

He turned his back on his brothers and closed his eyes. Dread mounted with each thump of his heart. He'd bound a soul. How could he have bound a soul?

Chapter Five

Cole entered the left hall beside the staircase and avoided the merry cherubs that lined the walls. His mother may have taken great care to decorate with ethereal elegance, but he could do without the cheer.

He paused as he reached for the light switch inside the study. The sheer movement sent him back to the family's arrival at Cornerstone Deep as his father had refused to allow magic for mundane actions. Then, however, it was the igniting of an oil lamp.

A lazy man uses magic for such things.

Cole flipped it on and grinned as he heard the switch *click.* Light poured from the circular chandeliers that hung from the high arched ceiling.

Veering right, he walked behind the oversized desk and scanned the shelves of ancient tomes. His gaze gravitated to the three crystal globes at the center; gifts to each son from the gods of Meridian—a rare honor, indeed. Upon receipt of the first, his parents knew they would be blessed with two more children. What greater call than to be a family destined to travel the realms as overseers, protectors of the gateway to the planes?

The crystals' iridescent surfaces gleamed. A mix of bitterness and reverence churned in his stomach. How could he have known their assignment to a Cornerstone realm would take over half their term of service? How could he have dreamed he'd meet his soul mate here in a dimension that offered no way for them to reunite? His heart ached for Meridian, his home, his repose. Yet, his soul cried for a miracle that would allow the rebirth of his love in this frigid world that bred cold, power-seeking hearts.

He placed his palm over the cool curve of his globe. It warmed and glowed at his touch. They had sat idle since before his father's death and would most likely stay that way. The Triad of Focus needed to call on the Trinity's power was unlikely sighting Vincent's temper. Cole scoffed at the thought. *Hotheaded irritant.*

He turned and ran a finger along the side of the cherry wood desk. Its smooth surface cast an unbroken aura, the spell cast by his mother to keep the furnishings protected holding strong. Her voice sang in his memory as she spent many warnings on Vincent. *"Things are so fragile here. You must learn to control your temper, young one."*

A snort rode his breath at the recollection. The words had only irritated Vincent more. To add to the annoyance, Cole had christened him with the nickname *Kid.*

The master's chair stood untouched. He'd never taken his place there when his father passed, feeling it required a rite of passage. Now however, the need to accept his position as Head of the Sentinels pressed on him with a weight of eternal consequences. He'd bound a soul and he knew as well as his brothers did that this time he'd gone too far.

A wide set of shelves framed the marble hearth along the east wall, displaying magical charms once owned by his father. From bulbous silver canisters to crystal vials, Cole knew each carefully placed one.

He stepped to the display and selected a shallow plinth topped with several golden circlets. His gaze flitted to the family's Candle Vignette and he paused. Picking up the beloved cylinder, small comfort lighted on his heart. He touched the intrusion at the top with his fingertip and a pulse of information crossed his mind.

Mianna Shilo, sixteen forty-two, second quarter, twenty-third day.

A smile touched his lips. Setting the items on the desk, he heaved a breath and took his rightful place in the master's chair. He passed a hand over the tripod plinth and the first golden circlet lifted, tilting back at an angle. The mirror within sparkled as the second level rose and clicked into position, making the two look like lazy spectacles. Once in place, the final circle leaned back, creating a tulip-shaped stage. The Utopian awaited his command.

A rumble rattled his throat as he pulled it closer. "Spying on a Grand Marshal's subject." *Disrespectful in the least.* But his brothers' rebuttals aside, his actions troubled him more than the concern for a lord's privacy.

Why the kiss?

He waved a finger at the instrument and the scene in the alley played forth above the circle of mirrors. She was frightened—a common reaction. He watched the crystallites mesmerize her and caused her to yield and breathe. Then she looked at him.

Cole flushed as he recalled the moment. A bid had touched his soul and he responded with a breath of awe. Threads of his existence tugged him to her and before he knew it, he lifted from the kiss.

It was like a homecoming, the taste of her tongue, its soft caress and sweet call. Time disappeared and in that moment, his spirit soared—and it resulted in the Zephyrus breeze of shared breath.

Cole glanced at the large tapestries of Meridian that hung on the wall beside him. Wasn't reincarnation limited to that gifted central realm? His experience in reality couldn't be possible—not here in Cornerstone Deep. Yet his experience matched the call of a reuniting.

Snatching the Vignette, he passed his hand over the instrument. An amber flame fluttered to life, a still life portrait undulating within its faded margin. He stared at the big blue eyes that gazed at him. How many times had he viewed it, that innocent face framed by long dark brown ringlets?

His gaze shifted to the harvest subject of the night before. The similarity was there. The way she looked into his soul was there.

A cold shard pierced his heart.

Dear Arylin, Goddess of Love. "It can't be."

Cole glanced up at the morning beams of sunlight as they poured through the gap in the drapery. He squinted away the sting in his tired eyes. His cheek felt numb where he'd braced it with his fist while he watched Anna's image sleep above the

Utopian. He dragged his hand over his face and then heaved a sigh. "I hate it when you do that."

"Do what?"

He glanced at the door. "Just appear there and stand watching."

James smiled. "I didn't just appear. I walked here and leaned on the door frame."

"Okay, I hate it when you just stand there and watch me."

"You've been in here all night."

"Is it that obvious?"

"Yes."

Cole wiped his hands over his head, smoothing his long hair. He pointed at a chair in front of the desk. "Have a seat. I need to talk to you."

James strolled over and sat down, lounging into the familiar counsel pose.

Despite his rash disposition of the evening before, he knew he could speak openly to this brother. In truth, his even-temperament was what kept the three Shilo brothers together. He waved at the door and it closed with a soft *click*. "Kid doesn't need to hear this."

"He's in the next room. Better to seal the study. *Eko silyst.*"

The air thickened and pressed on Cole's eardrums. Though it was the most secure form of communication, other than thought sharing, he wished James didn't rely on the charm as much as he did. But, years of practice didn't seem to help his lack of skill at telepathy.

Cole leaned his elbows on the desk. "About Lord Dressen's order."

"Yes?"

How do I explain this? "His calling for a curfew breaker as opposed to an individual in need of security."

"Yes." James set his elbows on his knees and pursed his lips.

A quirk tugged at Cole's cheek. "Then there was the requirement of total control."

"I assume it's due to the fact the subject was a law-breaker and he wanted to assure good behavior. But, I think it bothered Vincent the most. He never even considered what you did last night an option." He motioned to the Vignette on the desk. "Have you been consulting Father's chronicles? You know you won't find soul binding in any of them."

"No. I knew there would be nothing like that among them." Cole reached for the stout record keeper and passed a finger over the cleft. The picture of his love appeared in a flame.

James lowered his gaze. "Mianna."

Swallowing the swell in his throat, Cole looked at the cherubic face. "James, I never considered what I did last night an option either." As he looked at his brother, he sent his thought's voice to reinforce his spoken words. *"I didn't intentionally seal that spell."*

James' brow tightened.

"When she looked at me, I felt her soul call to me and I went to her. I didn't inhale the spell to seal it with a kiss. I took a breath to relieve the intense..." he lifted his hand, trying to find the right words. How could he explain the innate connection, the call of a familiar soul to another in a realm known to have no rebirth?

He shook his head and picked up the Vignette. "I kissed her, James. And when I did—*Gods*, I didn't want to stop. We shared a breath of Zephyrus, and it wasn't like anything I've experienced since..."

"Mianna."

Cole dragged his hand across his face and then looked James squarely in the eyes. "Take a close look at Mianna's picture."

James leaned over the desk and studied the innocent features of his past sister-in-law. He sighed and looked back at Cole.

"Now, look at the girl we just harvested." He passed a hand over the sleeping image and the scene in the alley appeared. Motioning with his index finger, he singled out Anna as she looked at him before the kiss.

James' features softened, but he met Cole with a resolute gaze. "No. That wasn't Mianna, Cole. You know that's not Mianna."

"No, James, I *don't* know." Cole shot to a stand and rubbed a hand across his chest. Hearing his contemplations aloud set anxiety in his heart and seemed to solidify the truth. He paced to the far end of the room, trying to settle the knots in his stomach. "I watched her all night. There are similarities. Things only she did, things so deeply ingrained that they're instinctive."

James stood and met him at the picture window. His head leaned to the side, compassion seeping from his emotions. "Cole, people do a lot of things similarly."

He allowed his heavy tone to accentuate his words. "Not these things." He marched back to the desk. "I'm not talking about how a woman tosses her hair or scratches her nose."

His lips curled into a sneer. "It's not unusual for a servant's position to evolve into mistress."

"No."

"And never has a Grand Marshal posted an order with intent of using the subject as a Chamber Maid."

James flushed. "No."

He stepped aside to allow James full view of the hologram. Blankets bunched as Lord Dressen rolled with his new servant and then buried his face in the waves at her neck. A low growl sounded from the reenactment.

Cole spoke through clinched teeth. "He went to her last night. The first night she was there."

James looked away.

"In her naïve state, he had his way with her. She responded just as you said. By pure instinct." He glanced at the couple then held up a hand to halt the movement. "I want you to look at this. And I want you to listen very closely to what she says."

Distaste flashed in James' eyes as he stepped to the desk. "Really, Cole."

Ignoring the aversion in his brother's tone, Cole lowered his finger to allow the scene to play forth. The innocent harvest subject threw her hands to her keeper's back, created a triangle with her fingers and thumbs. Her voice rang clear as she cried, *"Unsigh, Colhart!"*

Cole dropped his hand to brush along the desk. The image stilled and he looked at his brother.

James returned his gaze. "One heart, Cole."

"The spell I created for Mianna. The joining of emotions for shared passion. She kept it in her being all this time. Without realizing it, she recites a spell that will call on the passion of one man."

Levels of intertwined confusion, anger, sympathy, and shock emanated from James as he looked away. "You honestly think she used to be your wife."

Taken aback by the absurd question, Cole raked his fingers through his hair. "What do you mean *think*? Doesn't that just prove it?"

"Reincarnation doesn't exist in this dimension, Cole. Father tried for years to find Mother. She had to have heard those words somewhere."

"Father admitted himself it could have been because she held Meridian blood and we were in a foreign realm." He grabbed the Vignette, held it an inch from his brother's face. *"That's"* in his chronicles."

James lowered his gaze and set his hands on his waist. "Please don't break that. It's intricate."

Fire flared in Cole's gut and he grasped the magical album tighter to hold to his temper. He turned with a brittle huff and set the treasure back on the desk with a sharp *clunk*. "That's it? You're worried about how hard it will be to reassemble a picture album when... When I just bound the soul of the only woman I ever really loved."

"You can't think that way. Whatever happened, happened to a lawbreaker. Not the ghost of your memory." James straightened and met his gaze. "Father only searched for Mother because she *did* have Meridian blood. Her soul was born to a realm of rebirth. A Utopian would register it. Cornerstone Deep didn't allow her reincarnation."

"Do we really know that? All this time we believed it, but now I'm not convinced." He angled his head to emphasize his words. "I know that woman's soul called to me. And I know it was Mianna's."

"Don't do this to yourself. Don't add to your guilt of binding the soul by believing that it was hers. It wasn't. Mianna died long ago. She lived a full, meaningful life and loved you to the end. Remember her with love. Don't try to convince yourself Anna is an extension of your life with her."

Cole scowled and tore his gaze away. "I can't do that, James. You don't realize. It was too natural."

James heaved a sigh. "Okay. You can't set it aside. But, you have to take control of these feelings. You said it last night. What's done is done."

"You know by now I was just standing my ground against Kid. I didn't mean to bind her soul."

"What you said still holds true."

The words stung. Cole swallowed hard as a lump wedged in his throat.

James glanced at the door. "*Coneko silyst.*"

The room's atmosphere returned to its freedom as the silencing spell lifted. "Try to get some sleep. I'll check the remaining orders."

He left the room and abandonment filled Cole's heart. What did he expect from confiding in James anyway?

He looked back at the stilled scene over the Utopian. Wretched name for the instrument. There was nothing Utopian about it. It only showed his error. No matter what his brother's view of the matter, he knew what had happened. And he knew that his reaction bound the only soul that had ever touched his.

Cole picked up the instrument and stared at the image displayed. In his three life cycles, he'd truly only known one woman. One who spoke so clearly to his soul as to cause him to react on instinct that matched breathing.

Mianna.

He scowled at the Grand Marshal's obvious pleasure at having the girl and waved his hand at the sight. The scene faded.

Mumbled voices reached him from the hall and Cole widened his perception to pick up on the emotions surrounding the conversation.

Frustration, disgust. *Vincent.*

He listened harder.

"I felt that silencing spell lock the room like a tomb."

Pity. *James.* "Cole has some things he needs to work out."

"I bet he does."

"Okay. There's a new bid from Lord Craven for kitchen support and we need to settle on who to harvest for Dressen's stable worker bid."

Vincent sighed. "Last time I was at the park, I caught wind of a traveler hanging around. I'm meeting Elaina there. I'll check him out but you'll have to do a search for Lord Craven's. This guy didn't look like the cook type."

"You've been spending a lot of time with her. How serious is this getting?"

"Serious. I'm not like someone else I know who uses and leaves 'em. It'd help his disposition to have a steady relationship. But who listens to me?"

"He has his reasons."

A flood of appreciation warmed Cole at James' supportive words.

"James, this last woman is the longest I've seen him in a relationship since his last wife. Outliving them is just part of being who we are. Even if we're lucky to have real love for a few years before we lose it, it's worth it opposed to living life alone." The deep *whiz* of a jacket zipper sounded. "By the way, you seeing anyone? Other than escorting every beauty with hopes of snagging you from the nobles present, that is."

"I have an interest. But, I don't need advice from my little brother on how to love a woman."

"Right. How do I look?"

"I don't suppose you can do anything about that hair. So, you'll do."

Cole chuckled to himself.

"Can't help it if I was blessed with Father's good looks."

"Yeah, well, Father let his grow into waves and didn't leave it to look like Medusa."

In true Vincent fashion, his demeanor shifted from night to day. "Elaina doesn't seem to mind. Gives her something to play with."

"I don't need to know."

Vincent laughed. "I'm meeting her family today. Her sister's in town and they're having a gathering. I hear her father's quite an individual, so wish me luck."

"Luck."

Cole stepped into the hall to get a clearer sense of the discussion. If he knew him at all, this meant he was ready to further the relationship.

James stepped to the front door with Vincent. "Have you discussed anything with this girl yet?"

Vincent looked at him and his features softened. "She knows we manipulate the elements. I got her word of secrecy."

"You feel you can trust her?"

"I trust her, but I'm not stupid." He pulled a wristlet from his pocket. "I'm gifting her a promise band today."

"You are serious."

"She's the one, James. If she accepts the promising, I'm going to tell her everything. And I know she will." He ran his finger over the cluster of champagne diamonds imbedded in the gold band.

"Make sure she understands the binding before you place it on her wrist."

"I know how it all works. I've never had a problem with the women I've chosen." Vincent pocketed the treasure and turned for the door. "But don't worry. I'll cover it all. We'll stroll the park before we head over to meet her family. I'm sure there's a harvest subject there for Dressen."

"You have your scrying lens?"

He pulled up his jacket sleeve to show the blue sheen of tiny symbols on his watch. "Always."

Leaning into his step, Cole let his lazy stride clunk down the hall and then shuffled to a stop. "And where are you off to, Kid?"

Vincent spun to face him and held his arms wide. "To experience life's sweet love, brother. My heart is out there and I don't want to keep her waiting. So, I'd better be off."

James smiled, forcing his dimples to crease his cheeks, as Vincent bowed a gilded respect to the eldest of the house. With a flick of his hand, he dispersed into the Smoke of Night. The front door flung open and his essence shot out onto the sunny grounds as a dark cloud of dust.

Cole shouted after him. "Be back by dusk! We have work to do."

As Vincent circled the center fountain, a distinct sense of mockery flew through Cole. He glared and watched Kid dart across the yard and over the hedge toward town.

Chapter Six

Vincent stepped from behind the large oak and raked his fingers through his hair. Isles of multi-colored blooms lined the walkway of Shilo Park, welcoming the weekend visitors with a potpourri of spring offerings. Couples strolled along the red brick path hand-in-hand. A small family spread a large blanket on the fresh grass beside the stream. Birds sang and danced along the branches overhead while Center Creek gabbled on its way through the green.

He glanced at his watch and whispered, *"Bhiorus."* The luminescent face throbbed a muted glow and sent a pulse of acknowledgement across his mind. *Harvest search set.*

Launching into a jog, he dodged a pair of lazy walkers and then followed the footpath around a gentle bend. Elaina stood at the rise of Center Creek Bridge and he paused to take in the sight. A smile inched up his lips. Could it make a better scene for a storybook?

A cobbled arch stretched over the water with banisters of columned whinstone. Her lightly freckled complexion framed bright blue eyes and strawberry blonde curls tumbled down her slender back. As always, she wore a dress that screamed *I'm a modest young woman and as sweet as they come*. The charm tugged at Vincent's heart.

She held to the sand-colored handrail and gazed at the cloudless sky. With a squelch in her cheek, she looked down at her watch.

I'm late. I knew it. He shifted into a trot and then hopped along the outskirts of a group as he neared. Catching her waist from behind, she gasped as he spun her around and then pulled her into a kiss.

"Have you been waiting long?"

She sniggered. "Well, I was beginning to wonder."

"Sorry, family matters."

A twinkle caught her eye as she winked and then peered at him through her lashes. "Am I ever going to get to meet them?"

"Very soon. But, trust me we're just like any brothers living in the same house. Cole, moody. James, all-knowing." He smiled.

"There's more to them than that, I know it." She tilted her head to accentuate her obvious push of the subject. "Three wizards living in the city's most historical manor?"

Vincent glanced to his side. "Three brothers living in an old house."

"Uh, huh."

Time to tell her more than the simple fact he practiced *wizardry*, especially if he wanted their relationship to move forward—and that was exactly what he intended.

He took her hand, leading her to walk. "There are a few other things you need to know before you meet them."

She watched him as he searched for a place to begin.

"Elaina, being a Shilo...means more than just being born into a Founder's family. Our family is different. We have a role to fill."

Dipping his hand into his pocket, his fingers tapped the promise band. It should be on her wrist before he shared much more. His gaze flitted to hers. Presenting it to Elaina before he told her anything seemed like a blatant display of distrust. Her sensitive heart would be hurt, and the stars and planes knew it would tear him up to see that happen.

I can trust Elaina. I know it.

Leaving the bracelet stashed in his jacket, he let his hand swing at his side. He opened his mouth to begin and then caught the words before they hit the air. *Gods, why is it so much more difficult to tell her than the others?*

"What is it? Do they think I won't fit because I'm not a royal?"

Halting his stride, he turned to her and shook his head. "It's not that. But, you need to realize that what I tell you about my family has to stay between us."

Her light brows furrowed. "You can trust me, Vince. I'd never let you down."

He brushed her cheek with his fingertips. "Don't ever let me down, Elaina. You have no idea what that would do to me."

"I love you. Nothing you tell me about your family is going to change that."

"You were a little set back when I told you about the wizardry."

A breath of humor accentuated her words. "Who wouldn't be? But, honestly, it only makes you all the more special."

"My bloodline is foreign, Elaina. We're not from here." The words dropped from his lips like lead and he expected her to consider the comment. Her response came instantly.

"Well, your accent makes that kind of obvious." She smiled with a charm in her little wink. "It's beautiful. It only makes me love you more." Tilting her head, she sighed. "All our families came from somewhere before here."

"Elaina," Vincent placed his hands on her shoulders. She clearly didn't understand the gravity of the statement. "Have you ever met another who could cast spells?"

A laugh punctuated her answer. "No."

"So, where do you think I got this ability?"

"I imagine it's something certain people can develop. You know, like—you're probably more sensitive to your surroundings. Maybe."

Vincent shook his head. "I inherited it. It's prominent in my culture. All my people can manipulate the elements."

She folded her arms and looked to the side as if pondering the statement. "All your people? I don't know of a culture that performs magic."

He glanced along the walkway and paused, allowing a couple to stroll past. Not the best place to hold the conversation. Should he wait? His fingers flexed and then tapped his legs. Anxious energy buzzed around his stomach. *No. Today, before I meet her family.*

As he opened his mouth to reply, a pulse of information crossed his mind.

Harvest subject Charlie Lestinger, five feet one inch, age, seventy-two. Consider for stable hand, gardener, or electrician positions.

Vincent looked at his watch. Acronymic symbols lining the circumference turned green and shifted. He grimaced and glanced at her. "Don't kill me. I have to adjust something."

Sighing, Elaina stepped back and looked away. "You need to replace that watch if it keeps shocking you like that."

He cocked a brow and turned, passing his finger over the scrying lens. The image of a slight man seated on a park bench beside the stream appeared. Vincent scanned the grassy knoll on the other side of the creek. Spotting the subject, he faced his love with a smile. "I keep the watch. My father gave it to me."

Reclaiming her hand, they resumed their walk.

"Vince, where are you from? The more I think about it your accent really isn't like any I've heard before. And though I absolutely get lost in those eyes, I've never seen any that dark."

He looked at her questioning gaze and sucked in a deep breath. "We're from far away. It's not as far as you might think, but farther than anyone here has ever been. We have to guard our heritage strictly. We are very different from any one born to Terra."

"Um..." she quirked her hand. "I know you probably meant that to sound different, but *any one born to Terra*?"

Shuffling to a stop, he looked into her blue eyes. "We're not from Terra, Elaina."

She nodded once and squinched her cheek. "So, you're saying you're not from this planet."

He couldn't tell if she was about to laugh or cry by the expression on her face. It could have been sympathetic grace as she thought he was crazy enough to commit into an institution. "I didn't say I wasn't from this planet. Just Terra."

"Right. Well, Terra is a planet, Vince."

"Just as Meridian."

"So, you *are* saying, you're from a different planet."

"Same planet." His words trailed into a whisper as he watched her for a sign of panic. "Elaina, I'm from a different...dimension."

"Dimension."

"That's right. My home is Meridian. All people from the central realm hold powers similar to mine. It's oldest, original, sets at the center and inspires the other realms."

She glanced to the empty air. "I see. And we're in the Terra realm."

"Yes. Well, actually, Terra is a Cornerstone realm. Its position is called Cornerstone Deep. Your familiar name is Terra."

Another nod. "And we all take after Meridian."

"In a way. Inspiration echoes from the ancient souls and touches the younger, influencing much of the progression made."

"So we have you to thank for the stinky paper mills and cars."

"What?"

"Since, you know, your dimension inspires us. So all the other dimensions have paper mills and cars too?"

Humor puffed past his nostrils. "I guess you could say that, and yes. The cornerstone realms mirror each other, like the midway realms do. I'm sure they have a form of paper mill somewhere."

Vincent set his hands in his pocket, delighted at how quickly she seemed to take to the information. "The level of influence is effected by how far down the spectrum the position is."

"If we mirror them, is there a me there too?"

He paused as the odd question halted his explanation. "Well, no."

"Not much of a mirror."

"Um..." Her frank tone caught him off guard and he gazed at her with question.

"But you're not from any of those places."

Exaggerated innocence peered at him. *Okay, she's turned this into a game.* "No."

"And...your familiar is?"

He sighed and looked at the red brick path. "Champaign."

"And what's Champaign's mirror-place?"

"Champaign doesn't have a mirror dimension. It's at the center."

"I see."

"Elaina, no, you don't see." Cradling her face in his hands, Vincent shook his head. "This is completely new, and you don't believe it. If this is too much, tell me. I need to know you won't tell anyone."

Her playful tone melted. "No offense, but if I told anyone this, they'd think I was crazy."

A chuckle burst from his lips and he pulled her close. "You're right."

Elaina held to his jacket and laid her head on his shoulder. "Okay, Vince. Um, I want to believe you, but come on. This is really not believable, you know."

"Would it help if I gave you something from my home?"

Her gaze sparkled from the tops of her lashes and he grinned, withdrawing the champagne diamond band from his pocket. He placed it on her wrist, brushed his thumb along the gems. Tiny spangles followed his touch.

The delight in her eyes warmed his heart. "It's a Promise Band. A charm I want you to have." He cupped her hand with both of his. "It holds magical properties. Firstly, if after I explain its purposes and you accept it, it will become your link to our ways. It will testify of truth and untruth so you know in your heart and mind what you can trust. And when you hear things concerning our lives, it will ensure that you can't share them with those that aren't connected to our circle. If you start to speak of them, it will cause you to forget what you're talking about."

He leaned his head to watch for her response. "Accepting the Promise Circlet means you accept the promise of secrecy. Elaina, will you accept this Promise Band?"

A sweet laugh chimed from her lips. "Of course, I accept it."

Vincent smiled and kissed the adornment. It gently altered to hug her wrist and he looked into her lovely eyes. "Then, I promise to tell you the truth about my heritage. I'm from Meridian, a dimension at the center of the spectrum of realms. My people manipulate the elements. And Elaina, we have been here a very long time."

Elaina's nostrils flared as her gaze darted to the cherishment. "That's amazing. I could swear it just said—*truth*."

He nodded with a smile. "I'm twenty-four."

A scowl crunched her face. "Oh, no you're not. You're... Gods, you're thirteen hundred, seventy-five?"

"Tell me you love older men." He chuckled.

"Oh, Vince, you're amazing! I love you."

He framed her cheeks and kissed her lips. "Promise you'll think of me every time you look at it."

"I promise."

"Promise me you'll keep your promises to me."

She leaned her head against his palm and her eyes misted. "I promise," she whispered.

James settled into the chair in front of Cole's desk and reached for the Utopian. *Reincarnation.* He could think of little else since the conversation. It changed every view he had of death in Cornerstone Deep. Could it be possible that his father, a renowned realm traveler, had it wrong when he tried to search for their mother?

Perhaps these spirits stayed near the loving bosoms of their gods for a time before returning to continue their souls' progression. It would allow time for the God of Conformance to instruct. The Goddess of Love and God of Life could heal their souls from a lifetime of pain. But, their mother...

He turned the device absently in his hands. Perhaps, the instrument had been created to serve this plane only, to find the souls born here and couldn't pick up the advanced details of their kind. Who would know better than Cole if Mianna's soul had called to him?

He pinched his lips together and passed a hand over the circlets. The mirrors clicked into place.

James hesitated, remembering the family's elation when they'd received their first assignment together...and his disappointment. As much as he'd hoped to find a soul mate before that day, the gods hadn't granted his wish.

A smile touched his lips as he remembered the first vows he spoke. A precious, beautiful woman, he'd cherished the moments he had been given with Sarah, regardless of the fact their souls hadn't made the deepest connection possible.

Heaving a sigh, James softly spoke the command. "Essence trace simplex, rebirth. Sarah Timberlake Shilo."

An image of a woman with dark gray eyes, hair the color of sunshine, and porcelain-painted skin appeared above the tulip-shaped Utopian. His heart leapt. Before his senses could calm, a race of representations flashed before his eyes. He flushed as the calendar of her progressive spirit pulsed across his mind. *Gods, it's true. Rebirth exists here.*

He clinched his fists and held his breath as he eagerly watched for the final projection. The images stopped and the information relayed the final name. *Tiffiny Tillman Steward.*

Air puffed from his lips. She was an adult. Married, but an adult. He scooted closer to the edge of his seat as he couldn't control his excitement. Shooting to a stand, he swiveled to pace a large circle around the study. *Reincarnation exists on Cornerstone Deep!*

He halted before the mantel's shelves as his gaze fell to the family's Candle Vignette. "Oh," he whispered. "Mianna."

Dragging his palm across his chest, a heavy sigh issued from his lungs. The pain Cole faced was far worse than he had imagined.

Vincent passed a finger over his watch and the symbols at its circumference whirled. A miniature James appeared as if he'd waited for the trap to open in order to stick his head through. "I thought you were going to meet Elaina's family. Is everything okay?"

"Everything's fine. She just wanted to meet one of my brothers and I thought you were lesser of the two evils."

James chuckled. "Okay." He smiled at Elaina. "A pleasure to meet you. I trust since Vince has introduced us in such a way, we'll be meeting in person soon."

Elaina smiled and waved a shaky hand. "Yeah, I look forward to...meeting everyone."

With a nod, his hulky brother's head turned to face him. "All is well, then?"

Vincent put an arm around his love. "All is well, brother."

"Then if you don't mind, I have research."

As the image faded, Elaina stretched her back and braced her brow with her hand. Walking in a small circle, she looked back at Vincent with a sigh. She smiled, a congenial smile. Shivers traveled along his spine.

"I've shared a lot of information with you. Are you about to run?" He grinned, tempering the insecure twitch that played at his cheek.

"I knew you three were wizards. So, being able to call each other over your...watch shouldn't surprise me."

"And?"

Her gaze met his, uncertainty vivid in her eyes. A definite feeling of her searching the depths of his soul washed over him. He held a steady gaze and allowed silence to aid in her coming to terms with the knowledge he'd shared.

The moment seemed to stretch, holding still the approval of the world around him. The brook's gurgles gave no encouragement. The bird's melody held no contentment overhead, and the breeze that rustled their waves around their brows offered no reprieve.

Elaina's posture relaxed as she took his hand. "I accepted that you had powers. That you were different from any other man I've met. I knew there had to be more. It will take some sinking in, but," she leaned into him, lightly kissing his chin. "Vince, you are the most wonderful man. I hope someday I can prove how much you mean to me."

Pulling her into an embrace, he buried his face in her curls. "Oh, Elaina, be mine." He quickly reached into his pocket and grasped the small box he'd carried for over a week. If there had ever been a perfect time, this was it. He knelt before her on the brick path and opened the lid. "Drink from my cup. Be my wife. Be with me for the rest of your life."

Cat howls punched the air from Center Creek Bridge as a group of youths clapped their approval. He smiled at their exuberant urge for her to accept. "Well?"

Elaina held her hand to her mouth, but he could see the joy in her eyes. "Yes, Vincent, yes!"

Shooting to a stand, he slid the ring on her finger. Cheers erupted. As the crowd ran in their direction, he snatched her into his arms and pulled her into a kiss. The gaggle gathered around with *oohs*. Triumphant love overflowed his heart. She was to be his next wife and he could remember no greater joy in receiving an acceptance to his proposal. He loved Elaina; her caring heart, strong spirit, tender touch, and the depth of her gaze when she looked into his soul.

"Excuse me, but I'd like some time with my fiancé."

With congratulatory shrills the gathering departed. Elaina wrapped her arms around his waist and her smile glowed as she met his gaze. "I don't care where your family is from or that you're older than dirt," she added with a snigger. "Whatever you are makes you more special to me. I love you, and nothing's ever going to change that. Nothing."

Vincent looked over her lightly freckled nose, the strawberry locks that framed her ivory face, and then deep into her blue eyes. His love, his hopes, all his dreams culminated in the moment of her acceptance. She'd pledged her heart to him. Promised to accept his differences, and now that she knew the deepest secret—his alien heritage—everything else could fall into place.

His soul sang, and as he pulled her into a kiss, warm wafts of honey and licorice fell from his lips. His Breath of Zephyr bathed her in the sensual gift of his realm.

Elaina's knees weakened and he held her tighter, intensifying the moment.

"Oh, sweet Gods," she whispered. "What is that?"

He stroked her cheek with his fingertips. "My Zephyr. A gift meant only for you. It's a taste of home, Elaina. A taste of Champaign."

Chapter Seven

Cole slept in dreamscape's twilight where he wandered the orchard of brilliant white dressed trees. Streams of golden sunlight warmed his face and serenity rested in his soul. He relished the sweet scent of apricot blossoms with a deep breath.

His hair fluttered around his shoulders as a soft breeze seemed to whisper, "Follow." Blooms fell from the branches, whirling along a path through the arbors. Curiosity guided his steps.

The florets led him between the budded trees and the further he strode a sense of unease stole his repose. He emerged from the woodland to a wide clearing of amber sod. In the distance, a woman lay. Her hand rested over her dark hair. A wave of foreboding washed over him. He had to get to her.

He launched into a run, but stumbled as if lead weighed at his ankles. The sod morphed to mud, seeping around his boots, yet he clambered to reach her. The mud thickened to mire. Grasping for support, Cole crawled along the mucky surface, intent on keeping the woman in his sight.

She turned her head to watch him and as their gazes met, fear clutched his soul. Flower petals merrily danced past him and then cover her like a thick blanket of feathers. She lifted her hand to him.

In a haze of panic, he stretched forth his and fought through the bog to reach her.

Her blue eyes closed. White blossoms cloaked her face. The breeze died.

Finding solid ground, Cole ran full speed. The snow-white blooms lifted, ascending to the bright sun. In desperation, he lunged to take hold of her body. But the down flurried under his embrace, swirling upward and out from his grasp.

He scrambled to his feet and screamed to the heavens, releasing ages of pain for his lost love.

"Mianna!"

A deep voice echoed through the torrent of emotion, and Cole turned to his father's call.

"We must seal the portal."

In lingering grief, he darted for the forest, urgency driving his stride. With dreamer's omniscience, he understood the betrayal, the greedy intent, and the consequences the act would have on the spectrum of realms connected by the gateway.

The arbors slowly stretched their stand. Limbs snaked into gray mortar. Leaves palmed into heavy brick. The sulfured odor of the industrial west side thickened the air and then ebbed away as the city center of Shilo came into view.

Amidst the bustle of modern commercialism, horse-drawn carriages rambled and ghosts of Victorian couples strolled. Time warped in his panicked mind. 1207? 1612? 1943? He spun around, trying to make sense of the scene.

Grand Marshals flowed from the capitol's doors and filled the wide steps to the stately building.

Laughter rumbled through the air as they jeer in his direction. He recognized each—from the time of his father's death in 1647 to the present day.

Lord Dressen stepped to the forefront. Eyes as black as his own peered from the lawmaker's face. Cole stared back, unable to pull away from the piercing glare. Wafts of licorice filled him and his nerves froze, shocked by the scented call of his home realm.

Apricot blossoms fluttered past, breaking the hold and calling for his attention. The white downy petals bled to deep crimson and then whirled like fury, darting through the spacious court.

He dismissed the sardonic crowd from his mind, turned for the portal, and ran.

Structure turned abstract. Color hung suspended as if a puppeteer ruled the skies. Time echoed in muffled surges, and as distance closed on the sheer bluff that held the portal, the world condensed into a single moment.

It was over. The door locked.

His sight narrowed to his father's cape bound within the sealed barrier of rock. The air reeked of decomposition. The intrusive knowledge of complete death seized his mind. With but a few steps to reach the mark, Cole's knees gave way and hit the ground. His heart stopped. Thick darkness enveloped him. A heavy hum took his mind. Then nothing.

Cole shot out of bed, his heart hammering. Sweat dripped from his hair and stung his eyes as he threw his gaze around the room to gather his senses. Dim sunlight streamed through the crepe sheers of his window. The still atmosphere and steady tick from the old clock on the dresser seemed to mock him.

He dragged his palms down his face. As he lowered his hands, tremors took them. Irritated at his state, he stripped off his shirt and threw it to the floor.

It happened so long ago. He cursed himself for allowing the nightmares to return. He cursed the knowledge of rebirth he'd obtained. And most of all, he cursed the inability to control the helplessness it left him with.

The final scene hung heavy on his mind. Completely bound. Complete death. The urge to heave gripped him. He clutched his stomach with a shaky hand.

Once the body passed, could a bound soul move on to new life, or would it be tied to the remains buried in death?

The stench of rotting flesh flooded his memory. Dropping to his knees, he snatched his discarded shirt. He stuffed it in his mouth and released a cry that expelled every take of air in his body.

Cole numbly made his way down the long flight of stairs and turned to the parlor door. The room was bright, despite the dark furnishings of cherry wood and leather. Large bay windows framed a perfect spring afternoon. One of the large twin apricot trees stood to the left, an incredible likeness to the orchard in his dream. To the right an ornately designed belvedere sat among a pampered topiary laced with blooms.

He tore his gaze from the picturesque setting and settled it on the large portrait above the mantle. His father stared back at him with a baronial gaze and seemed to watch as his son took a seat in the chair facing the hearth.

He traced the strong features with his gaze. Having been the highest renowned cornerstone Sentinel, he knew the hazards of dealing with the polar differences that inhabited these critical positions in the spectrum. They homed the humblest heart as well as the belligerent power-hungry. *Greedy, self-seeking, supremacy.* It knotted Cole's senses. Their relentless pursuit of power had led them to the source of worlds beyond their own, and this ancient master had given his life to save the system from those who would devastate the order.

The portal.

He knew, just as his father had, the only answer was to close the gateway. But, Cole had no idea that it would take his father's essence to complete the sealing. He bitterly shifted his gaze to the items that shared the depiction. He grimaced. Gifts from the lords during Sylis Shilo's travels, all of them; trinkets that had held such meaning to him that he had anointed each with a special purpose.

The Moment Maker stood a proud six inches before his father. The spindle's polished silver surface gleamed bright in stark contrast to the dark indigo robe he wore, its base a thin coin edged with encrypted symbols.

A scoff crackled in Cole's throat. *Moment Maker. Who would want to stretch time further?*

A string of cerulean beads wound loosely from his father's wrist to shoulder, secured with a bejeweled broach. These, he called Mother Earth, after a previous assignment to Cornerstone Summit.

In his right hand, his father held a small box. It fit easily in his palm, the brushed copper bedding a crystal at the center of the lid. Cole focused on the item as its uses came to mind. The Memory Box held the ability to restore past moments in acute detail.

Stepping to the painting, he studied the little container. A sense of hope filled him. *Restores past experiences.* Determination swelled in his chest. He tapped his hand on the marble mantle and turned for the study.

A muted glow met him as he entered. James quickly waved his hand over the Utopian. As he slid it away to a side of the desk, Cole bypassed him and headed for the shelves above the hearth. James leaned back in his chair and casually laced his fingers over his waist.

Cole glanced over his shoulder. "Having any luck finding a subject for the stable worker order?"

"I think so."

He nodded and watched him a moment. With no further comment from James, he returned to his plan, scanning the selection of treasures. Picking up the small copper box, he ran his thumb over the crystal imbedded at its center. It glowed at his touch. Clenching it in his fist, he turned for his master's chair.

"You're not using the Vignette, are you? I need to consult Father's chronicles."

James leaned over the desk and pushed the viewer to his brother. "Did you get any sleep?"

A scoff rode his breath. "Yeah. Dreams be damned."

Cocking his grin, James leaned into a stand and then headed for the door. "Don't let this eat you up."

"Right."

As the latch clicked behind him, Cole reached for the Utopian. His brother's quick dimming of the imagery and lack of a wordy discourse on his progress were easy signs to read. James was hiding something. Passing his hand over the tool, he called up the last viewing. A woman appeared.

A woman?

He studied the forlorn face. Sunken pockets shadowed her gray eyes and a loose bun held her thin brown hair. Her pale visage reached through her lips, leaving a sickly appearance, and though creased and weary, he guessed her to be middle-aged.

"And who are you?" A pulse through his mind answered his whisper. *Tiffiny Steward. Five feet three inches, age, thirty-eight. Camer Street, North Side, Shilo.*

"Okay, Tiffiny. You're not a harvest subject. What's my brother up to?"

A list of searches filtered through his thoughts.

Essence trace simplex: Sarah Timberlake Shilo. Gaynor Thatcher Camp. Caroline Wordsworth Lanning. Priscilla Steenburgen. May Archer Wilman. Lillian Rustenburg French. Emma Crow Brown. Martha Irvin Smith. Stella Masterson Kern. Geneva Charleston Grabble. Tiffiny Tillman Steward.

Ah, Sarah's essence trace. A smile touched his lips at the memory of his brother's love for her. The fondness was evident, even if he had married since. "So, he does believe me."

Cole tapped his thumb on the desktop. Why hadn't *he* thought of checking the Utopian? He knew in his heart what he believed was true, but... He passed his hand over the instrument and raked his fingers over his scalp, as he couldn't hold back the anticipation. Visions of the past flashed before him and he flattened his palms on his thighs as if to brace himself.

Mianna Newton Shilo. Airabelle Gifford. Aquilla Newbury. Martha Hollister. Bethany Thatcher. Anna Sinclair.

Weighty realization hit him as he reviewed the information. Anna was indeed Mianna's reincarnated soul, the soul that had pledged eternity to his. *You were waiting for me to find you, to continue our promised future together. Gods, Mianna, I'm so sorry. I didn't know.*

"In all that time, you never married." His hushed voice bit deep into his understanding. Bunching his fingers into fist, Cole closed his eyes and lowered his head. *How could I not know?*

Lifting his gaze to peer at the angelic face, he voiced his firm vow. "I will get you back."

Chapter Eight

Elaina's panicked senses rushed through Vincent as they flew over the city disembodied. A twinge of regret edged him for his choice of travel and he tried to comfort her. *Not much further*. His thought and feelings were the best he could do under the circumstances.

He admitted that the Smoke of Night hadn't been completely necessary. They could have arrived a bit late to the gathering. But his elation at her acceptance had his excitement ruling his actions. He wanted her to experience every aspect of his life—from the Breath of Zephyrus to their common mode of travel. He hoped she understood the form of communication.

Darting into a dusty alley lined with backyard fences and shrubs, he selected the back entrance gate at her home. As they solidified, he held her head to his chest and kissed her wavy hair.

"Are you okay?"

"Oh. My. Gods." Her shaky words came out in punctuated emotion. She threw her hands around his waist and held him, her hands tracing small circular motions on his back as if making sure he was really there.

He peeked down at her. "We're in the alley behind your house. Just relax."

"Relax. Yeah, sure. You want me to relax." She took a constricted breath. "I just felt every temperature possible, every bug in the air go through me, and somehow I heard every—what was that anyway? Static?"

Vincent furrowed his brow. "Static? Hmm, did the static make you feel anything?"

She breathed a laugh. "Feel anything? It felt like static! Tingly. Electrical. Confusing!"

"No, what I meant was did it make you think anything?"

Elaina paused a moment and looked up at him with a quirked cheek. "Were you trying to talk to me? Is that what it was? I thought of, *Not much farther.* Or I could have been praying that!"

Vincent laughed and pulled her into a tight embrace. "I was telling you it wasn't much farther."

"Well, honestly, Vince. That is not my choice of travel. Keep that in mind, huh?"

"I'll do that." He couldn't keep from smiling and his heartfelt breath of love skimmed along her hair. "Do I get to meet your family?" He glanced around at the garbage bins hiding in the little nooks of the fence lines. "Or do we stand here waiting for the trash men to pick up the rubbish?"

Releasing him and taking a few shaky steps, she headed for the back gate. "Yeah, they're anxious to meet you. Especially Linda. She's my big sister. Has twin girls—don't feel obligated to let them crawl all over you. They're five."

Vincent cast her a sidelong glance. "Twins?"

She smiled. "Yeah, can you believe it? As rare as that is, she had twins. They were all over the news at the time. Seems the last twins born were nobles over sixty years ago." She unlatched the hitch. "Anyway, Mom's cooking up steaks on the deck. Jarrett's—well, he's Jarrett. Probably won't tear him away from the sports channel." Her hands fluttered in front of her. "And Dad—okay, don't let Dad get to you. He runs a big company and he's used to barking commands and being in charge. He can be a bit rough around the edges, but he's really a good dad."

Vincent grinned at the rattled sound of her jabbering and grabbed her shoulders before she stepped through the entrance. "Settle down." He wrapped his arms around them and kissed her neck. "There's solid ground beneath your feet and I'm right here." He nuzzled her ear and added with a whisper, "I promise I won't make you travel by Smoke of Night without warning next time."

Elaina cocked her head and half-laughed.

Closing the tall planked door behind him, Vincent scanned the lengthy yard, forsythia and honeysuckle. There wasn't any particular pattern for the yellow and white flora. That is, unless large clumps protecting clothes lines and electrical poles was a pattern. An old doghouse that looked like it gave up the fight was buried among a bushy mass. Long growths that homed along the fence on the left were charming, as were those at the corners of the wide redwood deck just off the back door. Over all, the foliage sent a sweet scent of "welcome home," and even cast a small bit of the serenity of Champaign. The fragrance was different but was as plentiful as in his home realm. He glanced at the yellow sun high in the sky. But still not Champaign.

The short spring grass stretched over the rather large backyard like a carpet of glistening moss.

"Dad insists on having the greenest lawn. The sprinklers haven't been off very long. Sorry for the wet feet."

Vincent glanced at the quirk on her face and then looked at his boots. Wet. He shook his foot. Chuckling, he slowly waved his finger and evaporated the moisture before them to provide a drier path.

Squeals and giggles drowned the chatter of tiny birds overhead. Two lively girls, their blonde ponytails positioned directly on top of their heads like fountains, darted in their direction. One stuffed a half-eaten sandwich in her mouth.

Mrs. Cantrell looked up from her steak-stabbing and closed the lid on the barbeque. She flashed the newcomers a hospitable smile and with the hand that held the fork waved them to come. "Have a seat. The steaks are done, and I was just helping Linda with the girls' plates."

The twosome darted past them and circled the hidden doghouse. "It looks like at least one has already made her choice of serving." He narrowed his eyes to catch sight of what she carried. "Peanut butter?"

Mrs. Cantrell grumbled under her breath. "Linda, Mechenzie got into the peanut butter again!"

Long beige blinds slid aside to allow a shapely woman to step out of the sliding doors. She tossed her blonde hair out of her face with a flick of her head and set a large bowl on the table. "I swear it's her only source of protein. Mandy, Mechenzie, stop chasing butterflies and take your seats. I've got baby carrots here. You can dip 'em in the peanut butter."

More squeals and one disappeared into the bush of honeysuckle. "No butterflies, Momma, sparkles!"

The other threw her gaze at her mother as if she'd done something against approval. "There aren't any sparkles. Mandy's just fibbing again."

Linda set her hands on her hips and cocked a half grin. "Just get over here."

Vincent furled his brow and leaned to Elaina. "Sparkles?"

She waved her hand in an *accept it* gesture. "They live in their own world half the time."

The two dashed up the wide redwood stairs onto the deck. Selecting a seat together, one grabbed a hand full of carrots and plopped the dip onto her plate. Small bites of ready-cut steak were pushed far aside. The mashed potatoes stayed, serving as a bunny head to hold several little carrots she'd stuck in the top like ears.

Elaina's mother wiped her hands on a towel and held one out to Vincent as they approached. "I'm Bethany, by the way." She motioned to the two sitting across from her. "This is Mandy and Mechenzie. Just a hint," she said with a wink. "About the only way to tell them apart is that Mechenzie's eyes are a bit dark. So don't let them try to fool you." She smiled and waved to their mother. "This is my eldest daughter, Linda."

"Nice to meet you all." He accepted their welcoming gestures. "I'm Vincent Shilo."

Linda chuckled and settled against the deck rail. Pulling out a thin cigarette, she lit it and took a heavy puff. "Vincent Shilo." She nodded and released a billow of smoke. "Yes, we've heard so much about you it's like we've known you for years."

The glass door slid open with a *thud*, giving way to a hefty man. His red hair was the hue of paprika and his dark blue eyes sat close together on each side of his arched nose. He briefly scanned Vincent.

"Mr. Cantrell, I'm Vincent Shilo." Vincent stepped to him and offered his hand.

Mr. Cantrell huffed and sat heavily in his chair. "It's about time we meet you. Six months of dating my daughter and you only show when food's set out on the table."

Mrs. Cantrell patted her husband's shoulder. "Now, Ben, Vincent is our guest." She smiled at Vincent. "You're all Elaina talks about. We'd love to have had you over sooner."

Lowering his hand, Vincent glanced at her. "Well, she's all I think about."

Linda sighed. "That's so romantic. Jarrett hasn't talked about me like that since the girls were born." She smiled, smashing her cigarette into an ashtray on the ledge, and then took a seat by the girls. "Of course, how can I really catch his attention when all I do is chase five-year-olds and clean?" She shrugged and looked at the man sitting on the other side of the sliding doors. Reflection of the back yard in the tall glass withheld the man's appearance, but it was obvious he lounged on the sofa with a can in his hand. "Sports manages to catch it, though."

Taking the seat beside Elaina, Vincent shook his head. "Watching your girls discover life is more exciting than sports."

Mrs. Cantrell's eyes sparkled. "You see, Linda. Not all men are like..." she thumbed at the house, "him." She set Ben's plate before him. "Your father would have been more involved if his work didn't keep him away."

Ben snorted a scoff. "Work. You bet I'd have rather been with you three. And now, my work load just got bigger. Had a no-show. It looks like I'll be finishing up the Dressen assignment on my own." He set his thick fists on the table and looked directly at Vincent. "And how many kids do you have? Elaina tells me you've been married."

The tone of his voice was far from congenial, more of an accusation, and Vincent grinned, having a ready explanation. "I'm a widower, Mr. Cantrell, and I haven't been blessed with children."

Bethany leaned her head to the side in a sympathetic gesture. "Oh, I'm so sorry, Vincent. And you're so young too."

"And how young would that be?" Ben had leaned an arm along the table and held a steak knife, serrated blade upward

Elaina took Vincent's hand. "Oh really, Daddy."

He huffed and stabbed at his steak as Bethany placed a plate in front of Vincent. "He's just the right age." She winked at him and slightly shook her head as if to say, 'never mind him'.

"So, Vincent, I hope you like steak. You get the largest piece since Ben and Jarrett could probably eat the whole grill if I let them."

Vincent smiled. "This is very gracious of you, Mrs. Cantrell."

Elaina glanced at his plate and shook her head. "Um, Mom, Vince doesn't eat much meat."

Ben growled. "What kind of man doesn't eat meat?" He stuffed his mouth with a sizable bite.

Mechenzie upped her face in a know-it-all smirk and picked a carrot off the top of her potato bunny's head. "Meat used to be alive." She peered at the tiny vegetable with regard. "You can't plant a piece of meat and grow another one. Another soul has to be born."

Vincent blinked, unable to hide his surprise. *This child is five?*

Her dark gray eyes looked directly at him and an overwhelming sense of almond hit his soul. Almond? Could it be her eye color? No. They were definitely gray, and didn't vary from his for an uncomfortable moment. He made himself look away.

Bethany waved a dismissing hand. "Kenzie doesn't like meat, either."

Linda laughed. "We have to keep all kinds of alternatives in the cupboards."

Vincent winked at the little one, attempting to cover his unease. "Peanut butter being among the most popular, I'd suspect."

Mechenzie smiled back at him. There it was again. The sense of Almond. He blinked away the gaze and forked at his salad. Smelling almond was nothing. But, feeling the sense of an aroma was unheard of on Terra. In truth, the sensation was limited to the center realm—and then only through kinship or favoritism as he had for Elaina. Heat rippled under his skin.

Pointing his fork at Vincent, Ben sneered and cocked his eye. "It's from living up at that manor on the south side. What decent folk live shrouded lives? I don't know one person who knows what goes on up that way. The few who take that windy road seem to forget what they were after to begin with. Then say they don't see a point to go back. Odd happenings if you ask me."

"Daddy!" Elaina's freckled cheeks turned red and her strawberry waves threatened to dip into the steak sauce as she leaned forward. "Vincent is a Founder's son! You don't talk that way about the Grand Marshals."

"Grand Marshals are all over the news, aren't they."

Linda rolled her eyes as she stood. "Really, Dad. They don't seek the spotlight so they're shrouded? Sounds like they like their privacy is all. The Founders hold just as much respect as the Lords do. Anyone who can keep an orchard blooming year round is worthy of respect right there. I love that hillside."

She slid the door aside. "Vincent, don't pay any attention to Dad. He doesn't mean half of what he says. And you don't have to eat the steak." Sighing, she stepped inside. "I'm going to try to drag Jarrett away long enough to eat with us."

"Don't tell him what I don't mean." Ben took a hefty slug of his tea and set the glass down with a *clunk*. Cutting another chunk of steak, he lowered his voice to a mumble. "A man that don't eat meat."

In an obvious attempt to change the subject, Bethany leaned across the table and grabbed the pitcher of tea. "I thought Anna was assigned to the Dressen order. She didn't show today?"

"No." His voice returned to its huffy regard and he chomped bitterly on his mouthful of food. "He asked for her specifically again. I made it clear to her how important it was. Deadline's the thirteenth and she doesn't show. You don't botch up a Grand Marshal's bid. Especially this one. There's too much riding on it." He swallowed and stuffed his mouth with potato salad.

Vincent's thoughts suddenly encompassed the subject of the previous night's harvesting. "Lord Dressen placed an important order with your company and requested a certain person?"

Ben quickly swallowed the mouthful of food before he commented. "Of course it was important. All of Lord Dressen's orders are and she's worked on enough of them to know it. But this one was urgent; had to be done on time."

"And he wanted Anna alone to do it."

Ben huffed. "Said he wouldn't accept anything else."

Vincent slowly set down his fork as he thought on the information. "Was it a big task?"

Ben peered at Vincent with a look of new interest. "Maybe not the largest, but most important. Said he'd sign us up for the new convention arena without taking other bids if this order was to his liking."

A block formed in Vincent's chest. "I bet she was working overtime then to get it done by the deadline."

"Sure, she was working overtime. We paid her good for it too. Promised her a big bonus at his acceptance of the project."

Discomfort ate at him and he picked up his fork, set it back down, and then chose to try a drink to settle the anxiety this new information brought him. Lightly setting the glass back on the table, he looked at his host. "Would she break curfew to make sure it would be completed on time?"

Ben furrowed his brow. "Never said. She just assured me it'd be done by the deadline." He lowered his meat filled fork and looked back at him. "You don't think she'd disappear. You know, like they say people do for that?"

"I just know that the Grand Marshals passed the new law."

Mrs. Cantrell lifted a hand to her lips. "Oh, my. Not Anna."

Ben leaned back in his chair and stretched his shoulders. His face fell and he turned slightly green.

Linda snarled as she stepped back onto the deck. "He won't budge. Elaina, would you pass the salad, I'll make him up a plate."

"Sure."

As Elaina lifted it to her sister, Linda's eyes flashed wide. "Elaina!"

She nearly dropped the food. "What?"

Linda snatched the bowl and then grabbed her sister's hand, holding it up to take a closer look. The pink diamond sparked on her finger. All eyes gravitated to the sizable cherishment.

Vincent couldn't hold back a smile. His heart instantly grasped the moment as every woman on the deck, including the twins, stretched for a better look.

Ben leaned a thick arm on the table and glared. "And when were you going to announce this turn of events?" Gruffness returned in his voice and his eyes narrowed with the tightening of his brow.

"Isn't it beautiful, Daddy?" Elaina beamed and struggled to wiggle her fingers in his direction under Linda's tight hold. "He just proposed today in the park. He wants me to drink from his cup!"

Bethany threw her gaze to Ben. "Oh! A Chalice wedding!" She grabbed hold of his sleeve. "Honey, do you realize what this means?"

"It means this boy doesn't even have the courtesy to speak to a girl's parents before approaching her on the matter. That's what this means!"

"Honestly, Ben. She's twenty-one." Bethany jumped from her chair. "Chalice weddings happen fast. We have so much to plan!"

Ben sent his glare to his wife. "What do you mean they happen fast? Now just wait one minute!"

"Dad, Chalice weddings are reserved for royalty." Linda tilted Elaina's hand, allowing the girls to see the ring better. "If both are of royal blood they can take as long as they want, but Elaina isn't. She's expected to stay with the groom's family until the ceremony."

Ben jumped to a stand, hands balled into fists. "What?" He gestured toward the south. "With him and his two brothers? Up there at that manor?" He marched to Vincent, Bethany rushing with him. "You're not taking my daughter off by herself to be with three men that nobody knows anything about!"

"Now, honey." Bethany lightly held his elbow as if not wanting to press too hard on his thick skin. Instead, she brushed her fingertips along the wiry hairs of his forearm.

A growl rumbled in his throat and he bared his teeth with a snarl.

Vincent stood and deliberately wrapped his fingers into a fist to control any instantaneous show of magical force. He stood at least a foot and a half taller than the man but appearance didn't seem to intimidate his betrothed's father in the least. Vincent fixed his eyes on the two beady ones staring him down.

Elaina gasped and scrambled to a stand. She wrapped her arms around Vincent's waist. He could feel her trembling and knew she must be worried about his magical ability, were this to escalate into a physical confrontation. "Daddy, please, I love him!"

Bethany peeked at Vincent and lowered her tone to a soothing melody, as if reasoning with a child. "These men are Royals, Ben. Royals. And Elaina loves him. She has a chance at a wonderful life. Don't take this from her."

The sliding back door wheeled open and a tall man leaned on the frame. He folded his arms and shook the long blond curls from his face. Taking a drink from his beer can, he snorted with a cocked grin. His blue eyes twinkled with amusement. "I don't know who's the stupidest here. Dad for standing up to a Royal or a kid standing up to Dad."

Vincent's blood rushed to his head at the use of the word *kid*. Small sparks danced in his cuffed fingers. With a steady voice, he held his temper and spoke to his future father-in-law. "Mr. Cantrell, it was an oversight on my part not to honor you as the head of your home and consult with you about my plans to propose to your daughter. I love her and I want her to be my wife.

"And I can understand your concern for Elaina's safety. As far as her coming to stay with us at the manor until the ceremony, it's common law. However, as Founders we have the option of a promising, which we've agreed to. This promising allows Elaina to choose to join us at the manor until the wedding or stay with her family. I assure you, I only want what's best for her. I'll leave the decision to her."

Ben lifted his layered chin and his glare eased. "Well, then." He pulled his pipe from his shirt pocket, turned and stuffed it with fresh tobacco. "It takes a big man to see where he's done wrong and own up to it." He lit the bowl and caused a few puffs to linger in the air. "So, when does this wedding have to take place?"

"I'll call the officiator and set the appointment. It should be within the month. There'll be no preparations to worry about. Only immediate family attends the Chalice ceremony. We'll take care of this event. There should be a celebration planned for the following week to announce the union. You may invite whomever you'd like to attend." He looked at Bethany. "We'll cover all expenses. I only ask you take care to request the best."

The door slammed as Jarrett retreated into the house and Linda quickly followed. Bethany threw her hands around Ben's neck and Vincent could have sworn he saw a grin on the man's face as she pressed a big kiss to his cheek.

Pulling Elaina aside, Vincent framed her face with his hands and smiled. "Now that I know you're to be mine, I don't want to wake up without you beside me. I want you at the manor," he breathed. He removed his watch and slipped it onto her wrist. "Call me. Just say my name and I'll answer. Do whatever you can to talk him into letting you stay."

Her blue eyes sparkled. "I'll start packing."

With a smile, he pulled her into a kiss. The twins giggled, throwing their hands over their mouths. "I'll let myself out the way we came in. But I'll send a car for you."

"I'll be waiting."

Vincent brushed the diamond ring with his thumb, relishing the fact it now belonged to her. He hopped down the redwood steps. Joy sent a spring to his steps as he walked across the mossy grass. The tiny birds above seemed to sing along with the elated rhythm of his heart. A soft breeze blew, lifting his waves to dance around his face.

Ben's voice drifted to him from a distance. "I'd better reassign the Dressen order. I just hope he accepts it even if Anna didn't complete it herself."

A sour knot clenched Vincent's stomach, hampering his enthusiasm. With all that had occurred *that* information had slipped far to the back of his mind.

Chapter Nine

Cole paced the length of the front porch with an irritated scowl. His spiked stride made audible his frustration and in his annoyance, he found pleasure in that fact. He cuffed at the folds of his cape as he made another turn and looked down the drive to the iron gates. Wide shadows thickened to blanket the grounds enclosed by the estate hedge of Shilo Manor. The sun dipped behind the city's tall buildings and cast an orange halo over the silhouetted skyline. Tiny lights that shown from the structures blinked out in observance of the curfew.

Dusk.

His scowl deepened to a sneer and he threw his disgust to the darkened turf. Vincent's mocking of his leadership cut into his gut like a thorn. *Undependable childish runt.* Thank the gods for James. He was admittedly the steadiest one in the family. How many times had Cole left comments with his father on the matter?

"I know more of you than you know of yourself."

It had been the only response Sylis Shilo would give on the topic. Regardless, Cole knew he could rely on James. He blinked at the thought and glanced at the door. *Where is James?*

He eased his glare as the latch turned and his brother joined him with Vincent's cloak folded over an arm.

"Where have you been hiding?"

"Just working in the lab. Relax."

Cole gritted his teeth. "I told him dusk."

"He's in love. Don't worry. There's no rule saying we have to harvest this early. We've got all night." James motioned to the gate. "There you go. Here at dusk."

Turning with a huff, Cole watched the youngest trot up the driveway and onto the landing. With the release of a quick breath, Vincent took his cloak from James.

"You left by Smoke of Night to get there quicker, but you take your time on foot to get back?"

Donning the cape, he glanced at the comment. "I had things to take care of. I made it didn't I? And you can congratulate me. I'm engaged to the most beautiful redhead in Shilo."

James smiled. "Well, congratulations. When will this girl be joining us?"

"Soon. But right now I need to talk to you about last night's harvest."

Cole bit back the urge to storm through the door and call off work for the night. "I'm not in the mood for another temper tantrum. We have work to do."

"This is important, Cole. He knew her. The girl."

He pinched his brow. "Who knew her?"

"Dressen. He set it up so she would break curfew. His order was so specific because he wanted her. And he used us to get her."

Irritation flared to anger and Cole closed the space between them with three lengthy strides. "He set it up?"

"She worked for Elaina's father. He said Dressen ordered a large task and would only accept her work on the assignment. She was putting in overtime to get it done."

Cole grabbed his cloak with a glower. "Let's get this harvesting done. I have plans to finalize."

Vincent flushed red and his hands glowed with instant rage. "That's it? You're worried about filling another of his orders?" Tossing a hand at the city, unrestrained sparks charged across his fingertips.

Cole offered no response to his comment.

Vincent punched the air and a pulse of energy flew the length of the porch. Blue lightning pierced the darkness, bursting a couple bracing columns with a resounding blast. Dust and splinters flew through the air and the eaves craned, whining in protest.

James quickly held up a hand, halting the motion. A swift flick of his wrist and the dismembered pillars whirled into place before the roof gave way.

"You're just going to ignore the fact that an innocent woman was manipulated to serve his want? She wasn't without a home, Cole. A life! And she only broke the law to satisfy his order." He raked his fingers through his hair and then threw his hand down to his side. Jets of fire gouged deep into the terra a few feet away. "If that doesn't faze you, you must realize that we were manipulated right along with her!"

Cole snarled and glowered at his brother, leaning close enough to make sure his breath fell on his face. "I want him more than you do."

"Right. That's why you're so eager to bring him another subject. Why would you care what happens to these people when he decides to cross the line?"

James set his hands on his waist. "You need to tell him, Cole."

"I'm not explaining myself to Kid."

"I think I know what you're considering."

Cole's nerves immediately eased at the possibility of having his brother's open concurrence.

James' large hand grasped his shoulder. "You've got my support and Vince would be a great help. We need to stick together on this."

Vincent folded his arms and glared at the two. "Okay. Spit it out. What's going on?"

"Cole didn't intentionally bind her soul. It was a reaction to the connection he felt to her."

"Oh. So, he just had to kiss her and add her to the list of women he's used. He compromised our principles and buried her!"

Thoughts of the conclusive nightmare flooded him. In a sickened rage he spat the truth to his youngest brother. "It's Mianna, Kid, Mianna! Her soul called to mine and I answered."

He threw his disgruntlement to the grounds. The shadows had deepened to the point he could barely make out the light marble that made up the seraphim fountains in the center of the court. Beyond that in Shilo City the devils hid in mansions six times the size of Shilo Manor filled with gold, silver, crystal, the finery of Terra's elite in every room.

Damned arrogant, self-seeking, pompous... The greedy vainglorious czars planned, schemed to take the meek, submissive, and naive to serve their never-ending thirst to rule. Cole gnashed his teeth so hard his brain pulsed. Working his fingers with tight flexes, he bound them into fists. He would never understand his father's draw to this plane, this people.

Keep them sedate. Keep them happy with their world, whatever it takes. And keep them from finding interest in what lies beyond the portal to the realms. That was the underlying rule here wasn't it? Protect the gateway. He had been successful for nearly four hundred years living by that rule. But now...

Soft splashes sang from the font with an uneven rhythm and the hint of mineral water scented the vicinity as the breeze died.

He heaved a sigh and turned back to the newly repaired verandah and his brothers. "I didn't know at the time it was Mianna. I only just confirmed it. I conducted an essence trace. It showed a perfect line. She never married in all that time—just as I never remarried...a true soul mate's course."

The color drain from Vincent's face. The whites of his eyes shown bigger than his onyx irises in the dim light from the porch lamp. Vincent's lowered voice reinforced his instant change of outlook. "There's reincarnation in this realm?"

A hush filled the front porch of Shilo Manor. A chilled breeze bathed them, ruffling their capes and sending apricot blossoms to dance along the landing.

James' voice subdued. "Tell me you're planning to get Mianna back, Cole."

He looked his brother in the eyes. "I'm going to get her back."

Vincent lowered his hands and shifted his stance. "What's the plan?"

"Dressen's birthday is just around the corner. The first step is presenting him with a special gift."

James shook his head. "Magic doesn't work on Nobles. You know that."

He smiled. "It does if they consent to it." He took the edge of his cape into his hand. "Now, let's get this harvest underway."

Disbelief shown on every inch of Vincent's being. "You're still going to fill his order knowing what he did?"

Grasping the rim of his cloak, James stepped to stand beside Cole. "If we stop filling Dressen's orders before we get Mianna back, he could get suspicious. He treats average servants well. There's no need to suspect he wouldn't do the same for this subject. Now, you located a homeless in the park. We can harvest him. He deserves food and shelter."

"Charlie." Vincent shook his head and took hold of his cape. "When I saw him today I had no idea what kind of man we'd be turning him over to."

With a flourishing wave, the three furled their capes and took on the Smoke of Night. A deep chill bit at their essences as they flew within the vapor over Center Creek. Motion along the bank caught Cole's attention and he watched as a scrawny man settled onto a park bench, tucking a disassembled newspaper around his shoulders.

"Charlie."

The little man's bony fingers crumpled the paper from his face. His bushy brows furrowed with the quirk of his cheek. He hesitated and then replaced the cover, cuddling into the pages again.

Assured they had found the right subject, Cole paused at the bridge. With a billow, James and Vincent took solid form at the same time he did. He leaned into his spiked stride and the two fell into place at his sides. The blanket of fog retreated with a swirl and then slowly swept across the embankment, brushing along the homeless man. Their heavy steps echoed through the urban green.

Charlie grabbed the paper from his head and shot to a sitting position. He gazed down the misty walkway and gathered a few pages of the disassembled newspaper. "Wha?"

The three emerged from the fogbank lighted only by the dim light in the distance. Their capes furled with their strides and Cole knew they must look like reapers from the afterlife to the man.

Charlie chuckled with a nervous lag. He stood and rumpled the newsprint in his arms. "I ain't lookin' for no trouble here, fellas. I ain't got nothin' you want." He held out the lot in his arms. "This here's just my blanket. But you can take it if you like."

James and Vincent halted, allowing Cole to take the last two steps to stand before him.

Charlie's lip quivered with his grin. "Look, mister. I d-don't want n-no trouble."

With a graceful motion, Cole lifted his hand and sent a silver mist into the medium. Sprightly flashes overtook the view.

Charlie's grin widened into a toothless smile. "Hey, that's really somethin'. You do a show around here?" He took a breath. "'Cause, that…would…"

The man's gaze changed from anxious to calm, and Cole sensed his eagerness to serve and belong. Cole leaned his head, studying the crinkled, kind face as hesitation seeped from his heart. By the waves of cherishment flowing from him, Cole realized Charlie had known love, cared for many, and now struggled with the decision to forget. It edged on overpowering the desire for safe haven.

"Charlie," he whispered to his mind. *"There's no need to cast aside the past. You need only submit a will to serve."*

As if dawning lit the old gent's thoughts, he lifted his gaze to Cole's. Concerns fled and serenity poured from his blue eyes. Contentment washed the deep wrinkles from his face as he surrendered his will to service to the lord.

Cole stepped to him and placed a hand on his shoulder. Newspaper pages scattered as he furled his cloak, dispersed Charlie and himself into the Smoke of Night, and then flew North. Dim lights fluttered along the quiet city streets—stingy offerings to guide those who dared venture out past curfew.

Cole seethed with the information given him. Dressen knew her. The more he thought on the fact, the more agitated he became.

A half-glance at the string of specialty shops they passed and he noted that one was left lighted. An odd sight in the mass of darkened windows. No doubt, there would be a curfew breaker later. He dismissed the violator and headed for the prestigious neighborhood of the elite.

Wide granite steps met them as they came to Lord Dressen's estate. The hound-faced servant quickly invited them in. "Good evening, sirs. I'll fetch the sire."

As they crossed the ingress, Vincent breathed a whisper. "Anna. Thank the gods."

Cole's gaze snapped to him and then followed his line of sight to the wide balcony of the second floor landing.

She stood near the center of the cathedral-sized stained-glass window, tracing the fine lines with her fingertips. Sparkling pins held her dark hair at her temples, allowing it to drape past her shoulders and flow down her back. The blue lounging gown she wore was barely visible beneath the ballooned wrap that, with the help of her angelic face, gave her the appearance of an ancient sculpture's subject.

His senses relaxed and a small smile touched his lips. He could call to her—just a call to have her look his way. Would she remember him? Would her soul recognize his despite the circumstances? His heart skipped at the thought.

Lord Dressen entered with a smile. Immediately, Cole's boiling hatred returned.

"Well, this order was filled rather quickly." The sire looked at Charlie and handed Cole an envelope. "The last one took some time."

Fire flashed in Vincent's eyes and Cole advanced obliquely, putting himself between the two to ward off any loss of temper. "I trust you are pleased with the results."

"Oh, I'm very pleased. She's more than I hoped for." Setting his hand at his belt, he met Cole's gaze. "I trust your invitation was received to my birthday celebration on the fourteenth."

"Yes."

"Tell me you'll attend. I had specialized items ordered for the occasion. It promises to be quite an evening."

Cole looked down at the city's lawmaker. For an older gentleman, he held his age well, slight graying at his temples, face free of heavy lines. If he hadn't known the man in Utopian's scene was Dressen, he would have guessed him much younger. Cole forced a smile, but Vincent responded.

"I trust nobody will be breaking curfew to attend."

A deep melodic chuckle tinted the air. "Nobody attending will have that worry."

Cole glanced at his youngest brother. *"Check your stand. We're not here to condemn."*

Vincent shuffled his feet and then redirected his gaze to the balcony and the stained-glass art display.

Cole paused before responding to the query. The last thing he wanted to do was give this lord the satisfaction of an eager acceptance, though he was definitely eager to attend. His gaze flitted to Anna who had noticed the conversation and turned, resting her hands on the balustrade. His heart thumped three hard beats. Blinking his gaze back to the lawgiver, he clasped his hands.

"Of course we'll attend. I've prepared a special gift. I look forward to presenting it to you."

Dressen's face lighted. "Prepared. I can't wait to see what the Wizards of Shilo Manor have prepared for my fifty-fifth birthday. I'm sure it will be magical."

"Indeed."

Cole sent his gaze to Charlie and in a moment's thought released him to his new keeper. Then, with no further comment, he cuffed at his cape and led the way out the door. The gift would definitely be special.

Chapter Ten

Anna peered down at the three in conversation with her keeper. Her gaze gravitated to the tall man who spoke. His dark hair flowed past his shoulders and lay over the black cloak he wore. Remembrance lighted her mind and she glided her fingertips along her lips. Licorice and cream wafted through her senses as sentiment touched her observance. A kiss. A breath of life. An adorned moment.

She stepped to the stairs as he turned to leave. Then, he was gone.

"Clair." The sire's deep voice tolled in her ears. "Charlie has joined the household. He will have a place with the stable hands. See to it he knows what's expected of him."

"Yes, sire."

Lord Dressen turned to leave and the ferrety woman motioned in the opposite direction. "Just follow me, love."

Anna watched her lead a scruffy little man to the hall. His friendly features showed through the overgrowth on his face. Crinkles cornered his eyes adding charm to the weathered visage. His thinned hair was tousled and he walked with a stiff gait, his short stature slightly bent.

"Anna."

She immediately looked to her lord's call and flushed as their eyes met.

"Prepare for bed. I'll be up shortly."

Heavenly purpose filled her, and she darted down the hall to her room. Throwing the door wide, she grabbed the nightgown laid out on the bed and ran through the small vanity to the bathroom.

The woman in the mirror ran the short length with her. *Not real. Only a reflection.* Clair told her so when she corrected her actions of the night before.

She stripped off her clothes and slipped into the tub. With a turn of the faucet, the stream of water bubbled up from the spout and cascaded over the marble ledge to the porcelain at her feet. She pulled her knees to her chest and waited for a suitable depth.

After a quick wash and rinse, she double-checked her hair for suds. She ran Clair's specific instructions through her mind. Wash thoroughly, rinse thoroughly, dry thoroughly, dress.

She bounded from the tub and grabbed a towel, running it over her body. She raked a comb through her hair and turned on the dryer, impatiently whirling it in all directions. Vibration from it ran up her arm and the tunneled whine was like a drill breaching her skull. Panic stung her nerves and in a fit of urgency she threw the tool to the floor. She dashed out the door and perched on the edge of her bed. Her gazed locked on the door latch.

Empty time filled the minutes and hazed her peripheral vision. A distant hum lulled her mind as her thoughts focused on the golden knob that would allow her sire's entrance.

The latch turned.

Anna jumped to her feet.

Lord Dressen entered, his black robe loosely tied at the waist. His lips teetered into a crooked smile as he scanned her appearance. "Anxious this time, are you?"

The deep song of his voice enveloped her senses and she blinked at him, riveted by the measure.

He sauntered to her. "Your eagerness is refreshing after the countless refusals, but..." He motioned to her. "I prefer to disrobe you myself."

Anna glanced at herself. She hadn't followed Claire's instructions completely. She ran her fingers down her gown-less stomach. No matter. Her keeper was there and his glorified presence lighted on her.

Motion of his halted stride caused the robe's fold to brush her thigh. With a fingertip, he skimmed the curve of her hip and then the length of her waist. He lowered his gaze and tilted his head as he traced her ribcage. The dip of her cleavage slowed his movement.

The tantalizing touch sent thrills across her nerves. Her breath hitched. She leaned into him, savoring his touch.

"I told you if you gave me a chance, you'd be back. You could have had this all along." His body crushed hers against the wall. Hot breath poured over her face. "I could have had this all along. All those years of being denied, enduring the gossip of others behind my back."

He combed his fingers through her unkempt hair and knotted them in the half dried locks. "I always get what I'm after, Anna. Soul mate or not, you were going to be mine."

Yanking her head to the side, his lips trailed along her shoulder until his low voice rumbled in her ear. "You do want me don't you, Anna."

She wilted and caught her breath. "Yes."

"Say it. You want me."

"I want you."

He tugged at her hair, harshly grating her head against the wall. "Say it again."

"I want you."

"Again!"

"I want you!"

Grabbing her hands, he pressed her fingers and thumbs together, positioning them to form a triad over his chest. He grit his teeth as he growled, "Just like last night. Say what you did last night."

As Anna took an exclamatory breath, a startling series of bursts sounded from the lavatory. A galvanized glow pulsed across the floor, lights flashed bright, and then died. Sparks burst through the air, piercing the darkness. White streaks branded her retinas. Like shattering glass, shock charged up her spine and down her arms to her fingertips. A wild shriek punched from her lungs. Flaying her arms, she shoved everything from her path as she jumped to the bed and scampered to the headboard.

Lord Dressen's voice boomed through the room. "What the hell!"

Anna's ears rang in the soundless aftermath. Her heart pounded and her chest heaved as she stared into the black void.

"Wait, what's that?"

She opened her eyes wider as if it would help her hear something over the thump of her heartbeat. Through the silence, soft splashes trickled.

A flashlight lit in Lord Dressen's hand as he slid the bed stand drawer closed. Deep shadows accentuated the crease over the bridge of his nose as his brows pinched together with his frown. He pointed the torch at the floor beyond the foot of the bed. Following the dark patch of water-soaked carpet to the vanity, a puzzled expression quirked his face. "You bathed before I came, didn't you?"

"Yes."

"And you didn't turn off the water?"

Anna blinked as she realized she hadn't. "No."

He aimed the light at her face. "Your hair's half dry. What did you do with the dryer?"

"I threw it down."

Lord Dressen looked sideways and a weak chuckle passed his lips. "You threw it down. And you flooded the bathroom." He peered back at her. "I guess they figured taking your common sense with your memory would insure compliance."

He tossed the light on the bed and then stepped to a safe portion of the floor. "I'm beginning to see what I'm dealing with." A long sigh hissed from his lips. "No matter. You'll be with me while in the presence of others. All people need to know is that I got you."

Opening the door a crack, he called down the hall for assistance. He tightened the tie around his waist and looked back at her. "I'll assign Clair as your aide. I can't have you electrifying yourself now that I have you. Stay there. I'll send her to help you move to a different room."

Anna scampered to the foot of the bed and grabbed the flashlight. Returning to the headboard, she pulled her thighs to her chest and rested her chin on her knees. The light created a soft halo on the ceiling as she wrapped her arms around her legs and clutched it to her shins.

The latch clicked behind him.

Chapter Eleven

Cole's laughter rang through the study door and echoed into the grand foyer. He leaned back into his master's chair and stretched his hands high above his head in jubilation. He watched the image of Lord Dressen close Anna's door and then as if by second thought reopen it and head down the hall. Anna's confused face dimmed as he waved a hand over the Utopian.

"That couldn't have gone better if I planned it myself." He looked to the ceiling. "Thank you, Arylin." He chuckled and shook his head. "This had to be a love intervention."

Vincent scoffed but smiled at him. "Go ahead, give a goddess the credit. But, I could have done it better, if you'd just let me."

"No, you'd destroy half the house and set the entire court of Grand Marshals against us."

"Okay, maybe I would."

James smiled and leaned back in his seat. "As much as you'd like to call vengeance on Dressen, this has to be handled with care."

Cole swiveled his chair to set a foot on his desk. "This needs to be done my way, Kid. Promise me you'll let me call the shots here."

Vincent nodded and leaned on the door jam. "This is your baby, big brother. But I'm right there when you need me. Anything to get your love life back on track."

Cole looked back at his younger brother. The countless years of standoffs had promised a showy confrontation between the two when Vincent heard of the reason behind the kiss. But instead, he seemed genuinely pleased. He brushed at his pant leg and grinned.

"I remember how you used to be, Cole. You weren't always a brooding self-centered prick."

"Right."

James chuckled.

"You know what I mean." Vincent's voice softened. "Mianna's death did something to you. You never moved on. You used to love life. Take in every moment. If there's a chance to get that back, I'm willing."

"Well, getting it back is how it's meant to be."

"Where reincarnation is a known fact and connections are easily recognized. Father never found Mother. He said he'd tried countless times." He glanced at the Vignette sitting on the desk. "I accepted that Cornerstone Deep didn't allow rebirth."

James lowered his gaze. "We all did."

"Why would he mislead us? He had to know."

Cole picked up the Vignette. "I don't think that was his intention. He mentioned it was possible that he couldn't find her because we were Meridian in a foreign realm. It may just be that the Utopian can't trace souls from across dimensions. Mianna's native to Terra."

Vincent furrowed his brow and frowned. "So, Mother could be out there somewhere? Here on Terra? Or would her soul have returned to Champaign? The portal was still operable then."

The thought unsettled Cole. "I don't know, Kid." He looked at his brother. With the marked age difference in the three's souls, their mother was often the one to guide Vincent while he and James took on responsibilities beside their father. Of course he'd hold a more tender spot for her memory.

James chuckled again and the air lightened with his humor. "Surely, she went back to Champaign. I think we'd have picked up on a five hundred year old witch hanging around."

Vincent smiled.

"So," Cole slid the Utopian across the desk toward him. "Anyone you wanting to look up before you take vows with this girl of yours? You might find Rachael or Abbey. Out of the twelve, you seemed particularly close to them."

Vincent looked down at his feet and sighed. "I can't do that to Elaina."

Cole nodded and pursed his lips. In all honesty, finding a soul mate was rare at Vincent's soul's young age. For most, several lifetimes pass before finding their true match. His question was meant as a respectful gesture to a fellow Meridian if not an attempt at kindness to his brother for showing support. "So she's a special one." He upped his brow. "You're putting a lot of trust in her. You proposed and she accepted. She should be under our roof right now."

James nodded but his sentiment was with Vincent. "She accepted the promising."

"A promising only goes so far. You both know that." Cole kicked his foot to the floor and leaned on the desk. "It may not allow her to speak openly about us, but it doesn't instill the loyalty of a Chalice ceremony. She could easily skirt around the subject and relay the same message."

Vincent folded his arms and leaned his head toward him accentuating his words. "I trust Elaina." He straightened. "But I ordered a car to pick her up in the morning. If I know her at all, she'll have convinced her father to allow it."

"Her father?"

Vincent cocked his head. "Her father's a bit difficult."

"Is he protective or just stubborn?"

"Haven't figured that out yet."

"Well, I plan on having Mianna here by the end of the week. If she worked for her father, chances are your girl's at least met her. She needs to be where we can keep tabs on her doings."

"You mean Anna."

"What?"

"You plan on having Anna here by the end of the week."

"Oh, right."

Vincent looked at Cole with a stern gaze. "She might hold Mianna's spirit, Cole, but she's still Anna."

"Vincent's right." James looked at him with the same regard. "When we unbind her soul—gods be willing we *can* unbind her soul, she'll have her own personality back. Tell me you'll accept her like that and not expect her to be someone else."

"I know how it all works."

Vincent's jaw set. "Even though reincarnation exists here, these people don't live by the same customs as Meridian."

Irritation rippled up Cole's chest. "And you know all about Meridian union customs?" Grabbing the Utopian, he held it up to emphasize his words. "Soul mate, Kid. Dressen said she was waiting for her soul mate." He set the instrument down with a *clunk* and leaned back in his chair, eyes narrowing. "She was looking for me. She never married in all those lifetimes. That's five long lives of loneliness, Kid. That's proof of a souls' union."

"She wasn't looking for you. She was waiting for a man she felt right with. It's how they think."

"Vincentor Shilomacj." Cole glowered as he spoke, emphasizing the fact that Kid had one forename to represented his single lifespan. "You're implying that in your whole first life cycle you've learned all about a soul mate's love."

James grimaced and Vincent looked away.

A twinge of regret hit Cole for throwing such a low blow in light of his brother's support. Vincent couldn't help he'd only lived one life. He shouldn't have used it as a weapon. He blinked and cocked his brow. But it'd always been a good one.

Vincent heaved a breath. "Okay, look. I know you've lived an accumulation of over twenty-eight thousand years in your three lifetimes and found your soul mate, just don't expect her to be like Mianna. Let Anna be herself."

"Worry more about your own woman."

"I told you. I trust Elaina. Completely. She's as close as I've ever come to knowing a soul's love, brother. If she's not the one, I don't want another."

Cole looked at him and then over to James. His own surprise reflected in his eyes. Was it truly possible that Kid had found his match? For Vincent, the brother who eagerly moved from the death of one wife to adding another to his life, this was a serious statement.

The room quieted as all seemed focused on eternal union. The air thickened. Cole glanced around as he noticed the change.

Soft white light enveloped them, creating an ellipse within the study. Atmospheric motion ceased and Cole immediately recognized the God of Life's spiritual presence within the aura. Taravaughn had stretched forth his immortal hands, and it meant one thing; they were being prepared to communicate through The Triad of Purpose.

Sugar air permeated Cole's being as the Goddess of Love entered the hallowed circle. Arylin's amber wisps gently swirled, spreading warmth, pressing on his soul with each pass.

Vincent moved to stand beside James. Their bodies washed out like weak holograms in the bright void. His jaw slacked and brow relaxed with a look of awe. Recognition flashed in James' eyes and he squared his shoulders, lifting his chin.

For the gods to call upon the Trinity to communicate at that moment, the message had to encompass the topic their hearts had turned to—reincarnation. There had to be more. He widened his perception to channel the manifestation of truth.

In a voice so deep it rattled Cole's soul, pure communication entered his mind as Gryffin spoke. "Rebirth is not unique to the central realm, but common throughout the spectrum."

Cole directed his internal response to the God of Conformance. *"Yes. As it is in Meridian, it is here. If so here, it must be in the other mirror dimensions."*

"All life is sacred."

"Yes. This was never questioned. Throughout the planes, life is a gift never to be taken."

"Agency must be upheld."

"Yes. Agency must be upheld."

"Agency must be upheld."

Cole paused. Surely the great god of judgment heard his thought's voice. It pressed harder on his mind and he repeated the covenant. *"Agency must be upheld, yes."*

"Agency must be upheld."

Confused by the reiteration of the statement, Cole paused to ponder.

Free agency.

Heat rushed up his neck and bloomed through his cheeks so hot that he knew his whitewashed image must have tinged red. Who had accepted the role to the harvest the meek and lowly for the tyrants? As Head of the Sentinels, he'd conformed with each new law passed, coloring the meanings of their call as overseers of the Cornerstone realm since his father had died. However dressed with good intent, he'd strengthened the spells to gain more control over those harvested. From the simple calming draughts used by their father, to total compliance ordered by Lord Dressen, he had conformed. To make it worse, he'd adapted the roll to echo the nobleman's greed and charged for the service, a needless gesture sighting money was meaningless and as plentiful as the dust surrounding them. He resisted the urge to spit the bitter thought from his mind.

Cole's own words struck his mind like a blunt sword. *"This falls under keeping the Grand Marshal's placid. It's their bid."*

He closed his eyes and swallowed the lump in his throat. How could he forget such a basic part of the covenant? What gave him the right to question the rights of a being? And what would possess him to believe only their dimension held the blessing of rebirth? Regardless of his father's inability to find their mother, how could they surmise that spiritual progression was withheld from souls of the other planes?

Cole pressed his palms to his brow and wiped them down his face to relieve the intensity of the revelation. They'd digressed to the point of defiling sacred rights. *How could it take the situation with my love to open our hearts enough to call on the Trinity through the Triad of Purpose?*

With deep conviction, Cole accepted the covenant anew. *"Yes. Agency must be upheld."*

As soon as the thought passed his mind, words as sharp as a razor's edge sliced through his heart. *"Gryffin knows of this by now. His silence on the matter proves this is no different from any other duty we perform."*

Remorse clenched Cole's stomach as his pompous comment plunged deep into his soul. Strength abandoned him in gelatinous waves. He dropped to his knees. His core burned like a lake of lava and he snatched a short intake to relieve his lungs. His chest heaved a sob in an attempt to be rid of the acidic reality of his actions.

"Gryffin, God of Conformance, strike me now! I had no right to assume thy judgment."

Warmth enveloped his body and caressed his skin like a downy blanket. Cole lifted his gaze to the blinding aura that surrounded them. Arylin's ambrosia essence lighted on him. How could he be comforted, forgiven of such an offense? He longed for punishment in the face of the gods' spiritual presence.

As the sugar air sweetened, Cole recognized the next step in the holy communication and quickly stood. He inhaled a deep breath to brace himself for the God of Love's overpowering reinforcement of truth.

Wisps of gold swirled around them as Arylin's spirit touched theirs. His heart pounded against his ribcage. Heat poured through him. Clenching his fingers, he concentrated on slow deep breaths to maintain control of his instinct to flee. The atmosphere grew thicker. His skin seemed too tight for his soul.

Another deep breath. He swallowed hard.

Vincent gasped and doubled over. James braced his shoulders and he spoke in a hushed, reverent tone. "Arylin's bearing witness, Vince. Don't fight it."

Nodding, Kid straightened and heaved a deep breath. His hands trembled as he forced them into fists.

James looked at Cole. Conviction was clear in his countenance and the venerations that poured from him. "Changes will be made," he whispered.

Cole's nostrils flared as he forced composure and then nodded. "Changes will be made."

At his words, the air lightened, easing the pressure that filled the ellipse. The brilliant halo faded, color returned to their forms. The golden mist ebbed.

Cole looked from one brother to the other. Neither spoke, but emotions emitted from them in a torrent—James, shame and determination, Vincent, a mix of shock, awe, and pride.

He looked at his youngest brother with regard. He'd never experienced a Triad of Purpose communication. Their father always deemed his soul too young. A new light dawned in Cole's heart. A soul mate and a Trinity revelation in his first life? Perhaps *Kid* wasn't the best nickname for him after all.

Chapter Twelve

Cole swung his feet over the side of the bed as the old clock sang its sixth chime. He dragged his hand down his face. *Wretched dream.* How many times would he have to relive it? Mianna's shrouded body. His father's panicked call. Dressen's black eyes. And why the scent of licorice? He was fortunate the clock woke him before the nightmare revealed his father's fate—though he knew the outcome.

His breath puffed from his lips. He was more tired than if he'd stayed awake.

A pulse crossed his mind and he scowled as he looked at his watch. Vincent's bright image appeared as a perfect hologram over the luminescent face.

Cole grumbled. "Do you have any idea what time it is?"

"I'm looking at my watch. What do you think? It's six o'clock. Get up. Elaina will be joining us today."

"You work fast."

"Dressen's party is tomorrow. It'd mean the world to her to attend. I want to introduce her as my fiancé and most of the noblemen will expect her to be at the manor regardless of us being Founders." He motioned behind him. "I arranged for the officiator to meet with her family there. He'll explain things and convince them to have her stay. I ordered a car to wait for them."

A low grunt rumbled in Cole's throat.

"We're taking the master bedroom on the third floor. Chill a bottle of Ambrosia and set it on the table with glasses and have roses delivered and petals sprinkled on the bed."

"Okay, okay. Just hold on." Cole sat up and smoothed back his hair. "I have work to do. James can do that." His mumbled words fell limp through the air and Vincent's hologram nodded.

"Do I need to talk to James myself?"

"No, I got it!" With a huff, Cole waved his hand and closed the connection.

The scent of fresh coffee and quick bread met Cole as he lazily walked down the hall to the kitchen. The aroma of pleasant wishes filled the room that easily was home to every convenience available, despite their rare use. Silver appliances dotted the walls above a glistening marble counter. A large baker's island stood center stage beneath a rack of hanging cookware. Morning sunrays streamed through the picture window that filled the east wall of the breakfast nook, its intense brilliance reflected off everything.

He squinted at the brightness and glowered. Waving his hand, a dark opalescent sheen covered the glass.

James glanced up at the newly pearlized surface and then over to him. "Fresh muffins here if you're interested."

Cole pulled out a chair, cocking it to the side and sat. Leaning back, he stretched his long legs in front of him and set an elbow on the table. "Kid's made arrangements to have that girl here today. He's having it recorded by an officiator. Wants you to get things ready."

James furled his brow and took a bite of his toast. "It looks like he's fallen for her more than I expected. I have to admit, his comment about her caught me off guard."

Cole puckered his expression. "He was always eager to move on. One more notch on the belt." With a flick of his wrist, a mug shot to his hand. He poured himself coffee from the percolator. "Pass the cream."

"I'm sure we all displayed a bit of free spirit during our first life cycle. He treats his women well enough."

"And the butter."

James handed the items to him. "But to claim his commitment to this one after moving on when the others passed—he broke his own pattern."

"I'd say," Cole spread a thick layer of butter on his muffin, "our little brother's soul was created to serve a bigger purpose than we expected."

"That, coming from you is quite a statement."

"The gods accepted him as part of the Triad in his first lifetime. What would you think?"

"Exactly the same thing. It just sounds more monumental coming from you."

Cole chuckled. "I still don't think I can give up the fact that he's a kid."

James smiled and then waved his hand through the air, taking in the kitchen at large.

The oven turned on. Bowls, cooking utensils, and ingredients flew from the cupboards and lighted on the baker's island. Flour neatly poured into the sieve as the other dried products measured their respective amounts into a bowl. Eggs cracked and slumped into the liquids; a whisk beat the mixture at high speed.

He glanced at Cole's perplexed gaze. "I can't have guests over for a promising without refreshments."

Cole took a bite of his muffin and shook his head. "I'll never figure out how you can do so many things at once."

"Well, I don't see how you can pick up on emotions like you do. And I still haven't mastered thought sharing."

"You and Kid just talk too much. You don't exercise the inner process."

James chuckled. "Vince would say it's your brooding taking over."

"My brooding." He clicked the inside of his cheek and then took a drink of coffee. "My brooding has its advantages. At least I'm not going on wife thirteen."

"No." James lowered his gaze and sat back in his chair. "With only seven wives in nearly eight hundred years, nobody can say you don't take that step seriously."

"As do you, brother." Cole lifted his cup in salute. "So. How about you?" He took the chance James might reveal his essence trace of the other night. "Any thoughts on looking up someone? Sarah maybe?"

"I've thought about it."

He nodded when no further comment came. "Okay. Well, I need the lab to perform the next level of enchantments on the memory box. You won't need it will you?"

James gestured with his hand. "Go ahead. What I'm doing can wait."

Cole stood as the oven door opened and swallowed three pans of batter. Bowls and utensils flew to the sink, and ingredients returned to their proper place. He glanced back at his brother just as the bright stream of sunlight poured back through the charm-released window. Squinting from the glare, he grumbled under his breath and turned to leave.

Lab. Give me the dark dank lab.

Vincent trotted up Shilo Hillside drive, allowing the crisp breeze to wash along his skin. The gradual two-mile climb to the manor offered a picturesque view. Apricot orchards filled the border, suburbs skirted the park, and the east side merchants' district sprawled across the scene to the left. Industrial sites that towered over the trees silhouetted nicely at dusk. The heart of the city with its glass and granite buildings reached the butt of the mountain that edged Oberon Sea. Steam from the west side manufacturing plants seeped from the bluffs, where they nested to take advantage of natural ores.

Shivers sent tingles to dance across Vincent's arms and up his neck with each forward bound. Twitching his finger, the wide gates to Shilo Manor swung open. He entered the plush grounds with a skip. The iron bars clanked shut behind him.

Elaina's call pulsed across his mind. He paused and looked down at his watch with a smile. "Tell me you're ready."

"This is so amazing! I can see you so clearly." She beamed up at him from the face of the instrument. "And you sent a Nobleman's limo? The neighbors keep calling Dad to see what's going on. He's beside himself." She lowered her tone to mimic her father's voice. "My daughter's marrying a royal Founder's son. She has certain privileges now, you know."

"Well, I want your family to come to the manor today. An officiator is going to record the promising and explain a few things. It should set his mind at ease concerning your stay with us."

Elaina laughed. "Oh, they'll like that. Imagine, my family in a wizard's home."

"What was that, dear?"

Vincent scowled. "Who was that?"

"Oh, Mom's gathering things from her wedding. I'm going to wear her gown. Kind of a tradition. She's getting it ready for the cleaners."

A chill stabbed his senses. "Elaina." He spoke in a hushed voice. "You haven't said anything remotely near what we're about, have you? She doesn't know of the scrying lens I gave you does she?"

"Huh? No, of course not." She glanced over to her mother. "She didn't really hear me." She gave a little shake of her head in that direction.

Vincent closed his eyes and took a steady breath. Foreboding crossed his heart. "What about your father."

"No. Vince, I wouldn't tell anyone."

"You just said it in front of your mother, Elaina!"

"It slipped out. And really, she—didn't catch it."

Raking his fingers over his head, he growled and threw his hand down to his side. Blue neon bolted from his fist, gouging into the drive. Cobblestones shot through the air from the strike.

"Make sure she says *nothing*," he hissed. "You don't *realize* the severity of disclosing that information!"

"Okay, Vince, I promise." Tears welled in her eyes.

His heart sank at the sight. "Aw, Elaina, I'm sorry—silence is paramount. You'll grow to understand as you learn more, but for now please tell me you'll be more careful in honoring the promising. You may not be able to speak out directly, but information can get relayed."

Elaina's face melted and her glistening eyes sought his. "I promise, Vince. I promise. I'm so sorry it slipped. I love you."

"I love you, too. Just get here as soon as you can. And—be sure the whole family comes."

"Linda and Jarrett left last night with the girls. He refused to stay another day. But Mom and Dad will be there."

He nodded and offered a small smile. "I'll be here waiting." He dropped his hand, closing the connection and ran his fingers through his hair. Turning toward the manor, he stormed through the door. "Cole!"

James' voice came from the kitchen. "He's in the lab."

With a determined stride, he headed down the hall, taking the first door to the left.

Cole called up his father's chronicles and passed a finger over the Vignette's flame as if turning the pages to a book. As the appropriate instructions appeared, he retrieved the small memory box from his pocket. Its copper surface gleamed brightly with the effects of his last level of enchantments and satisfaction lightened his mood. It appeared just as it should.

He performed the next step of the charm, whispering incantations as his hand re-created the ritual depicted in the images. The crystal center glowed and the delicate etchings altered.

Cole smiled as the door to the lab opened and steps descended the hardwood stairs into the basement. He held up his hand to ward off speech as Vincent came into view.

He whispered another spell, producing a fine mist of lavender to hover over a shallow bowl. He pinched at the cloud and led a trail of quintessence to the memory box as he continued his recital. *"Merromel estora, consentrae allure."* Holding his hand level with the container, a puff of ginger fell from his palm to the contents. *"Cloer disantan omeret, amid emoria tress."*

He closed the jewel-crested lid and sighed. "It's complete. Knowing Dressen, he won't be able to refuse."

Vincent nodded and motioned to the box. "You called for the enhancement of his experiences when he relives the memories he focuses on." He smiled. "And did I catch the word desire in there too?"

"This is a gift he'll have a hard time putting down." Cole dimmed the Vignette's instructions. "James has been working in the kitchen to welcome our guests. When are they showing?"

"The limo's waiting for them. And, I think we'd better present the family with promise bands."

Cole glared at him. "Why? What happened?"

"When Elaina called, she mentioned our being wizards with her mother in the room."

"What?" He shot to a stand and paced the length of the lab. "How many other times has she just *mentioned* we were wizards with someone around?"

"Don't get bent, there."

Cole stormed to Vincent, pointing an accusing finger at his chest. "This is on you. They accept a full promising of their own will or I'll take care of it *my* way. We will not be disclosed by a loose-tongued fem." He headed for the stairs.

"There might be a slight problem with her father. He likes to be in charge. He might consent if we play him right but I doubt his heart will be in it."

Cole stomped up the steps. "Or *my* way, Kid!"

Chapter Thirteen

Anna watched as bright light rippled along Clair's long hair. She reached out and brushed at the dark tresses.

The little lady glanced over her shoulder and her tiny lips curved upward. "Anna, love, that's the third time you've brushed at my hair. I can wear it down all the time if you like it this way." She looped a lock behind her ear. "I usually put it in a bun when I help in the kitchen, but since I've been assigned as your guide, there's no need."

Anna smiled. "It's so pretty. And soft."

"Oh, you are a sweet one."

Rounding the corner onto the second floor landing, the hound-faced man came to view. Of all the servants Lord Dressen employed, he was amazing. Tall, lanky, slicked hair, and the most emotionless until...

He glanced their way and his droopy visage came to life. Anna's heart danced at the change.

"Clair, my sweet," his soft voice sang.

"Reg, that banister has been polished a million times. The maids do a fine job. There's no need for your bother."

"There's nothing wrong with my bothering. It's my pleasure to attend to the sire's house." Turning to the large stained-glass window, he tugged another rag from his shoulder and dusted at the geometric shapes.

The colorful montage grasped Anna's attention. Something about them called to her soul, called her home.

"You showing our new girl the...?"

Clair responded with a *shush*. "It's a surprise. Now you hush."

A pause in the conversation allowed Anna to wrap around the shapes again, but Clair's whisper interrupted.

"I've never seen the likes. Just look at her, lost to the world. Reg, that girl is the sweetest thing ever to join the household. But... Something's not right with her. It's like she's not all there. I wonder how deeply she chose to forget her past. Not even recognizing her own reflection?"

"Do you ever regret electing to forget, my little Clair?"

"Only very few times. But, I had to want it or it wouldn't stay hidden, isn't that right? I always fall short of searching my mind for the hidden. I'm afraid now to know what it was like. I'm happy here, feel like I belong. We're family and I wouldn't change that one bit."

"And I'm glad." Fabric rustled behind her, suggesting the two embraced. "A better friend I've never had in all my years of service to the sire."

"Another reason I don't even try to remember."

A low sigh accompanied more fabric rustles and Reg spoke. "It's a good thing the sire has taken to her so. I don't think I've ever seen him personal with an addition."

Humor tinted Clair's quiet voice. "I know of at least six maids under this roof that are jealous beyond civil over it, too. I warned them to just keep their distance or they'd have us to deal with."

Reg's deep chuckle tickled Anna's ears. "The mention of scrapping with you would keep them away, my sweet Clair. Lord Dressen chose right when he assigned you as her personal aide."

"Ooh, well, she deserves looking after." Clair stepped to Anna's side and looked up at the stained-glass. "This is one of Lord Dressen's favorite works. He had it commissioned. Talented artist. Filled it to his specification. Isn't it lovely?"

Anna nodded and ran her fingers over the lead that held the intricate shapes together. "It's beautiful."

"Well, if you like this, you'll love what's down the hall. It's like a cathedral."

She reluctantly pulled her gaze away to face her guide. Little eyes sparkled back at her like shiny gems beneath the ceiling's many pin lights.

Motioning down the hall, Clair took Anna's hand and led the way. "I wanted to show it to you yesterday, but other duties got in the way. It took months to renovate. Don't know how he got the people to part with the items. They've been kept by the Arylin Colony in the Northern Territory. The only one of its kind. But he got them. He does have his ways." She winked. "I told you that you were a special one. He said that the woman that filled this post would enjoy it more than any other room in the house."

Clair turned on the light as they entered. A soft glow haloed the laurel sconces at the center of each gold-trimmed panel lining the walls. Positioned beneath the illuminations, six red velvet divans sat, matching the wide runner that covered the marble floor and led to the end of the room. Amber pillars with deep golden veins stood in the far corners and flanked an ivory statue at center stage. Beams poured from the spotlights in the base, highlighting the eight foot tall being, and reflecting off the wall mirror behind it. An ivory-laced prie-dieu humbly sat before the pedestal.

"He's having stained-glass screens made. It will give you more privacy when you worship."

Blood drained from Anna's face as she gazed at the Goddess of Love. The gentle eyes beckoned her from a smooth alabaster visage. Long waves flowed, crowned with a brow band that fanned along the sides of her head. Her arms seem to lift in welcome, her silk robes furling at her sides and down her slender body to brush the plinth.

Time locked in a surreal moment. Anna's feet moved, carrying her down the long carpet that lead to her goddess. Her heart raced and supplication bloomed across her nerves. She broke into a run.

Throwing herself onto the stand, she grasped at the white flowing robe. She scrambled up the length of Arylin's body and reached for the angelic face. Her fingertips merely brushed along the mane of intricate feathers that adorned her shoulders.

Clair's little shoes tip-taped toward her until the runner muffled the sound. "Oh, Anna, dear. This is only a statue of Arylin."

Anna gazed high in adoration. "My goddess."

Distorted thoughts fluxed through her mind, distant chants, familiar song, then gone. Heat bore into her temples with each ebb, sending pulses down her jaw to circle her neck and chest. Invisible cords snaked through her torso, wrapping tightly around her lungs and abdomen. Tiny spars spangled along the threads singeing her core. She knotted a fist to her bosom as a wail rattled deep in her chest.

Shock squelched from Clair's voice. "Anna!"

Anna clawed at the bodice of her gown, desperate to reveal the binds that burned her soul. Dropping to her knees, strained whispers passed her lips.

> "Arylin, Goddess of Love,
> grace forsake me not.
> Guile and torment take my heart,
> cast me not this fate.
> Holy be thy name.
> Holy be thy name!"

"Reg! Reg, come quick!" Claire brushed Anna's strewn hair from her face and tried to inch the gown back around her body. "It's okay, love. It's all going to be okay." She gently grasped Anna's arms, tugging her away from the goddess. Tremors rode her words. "We can visit another time. All of this seems a bit much for you."

Anna lunged for the Arylin's legs, hooking her fingers around the stony folds.

"What seems to be the problem?"

The deep voice echoed through the room and penetrated Anna's heart. She threw her gaze to the entrance and her jaw dropped in awe as Lord Dressen strode in her direction. Pain melted in a heated wash. Her hands dropped from the rock. His dark eyes flashed, heavy brows dipped low, and they were the most majestic things she'd ever seen. Fears disappeared.

"She just went off, sire. Beats all I've seen. She screamed and started reciting...a prayer, I think."

Lord Dressen eased to sit on the platform and he gently framed her face. "Anna," he said softly.

She rested her cheek in his large palm and a shaky sigh relieved her lungs. Pangs spangled through her veins, but she didn't care. His touch, his being, caressed her soul with comfort.

Lord Dressen's hands slowly dropped and wrapped around hers. "Come with me."

Gazes locked, he guided her to stand and led the way out of the room and into the hall. Each backward step, she matched in forward motion. He leaned his head. She leaned hers. They followed the long trail, passing the stained-glass window wall. Servants paused on the steps and quietly watched.

Dressen brushed the disheveled hair from Anna's face. "The shrine was meant as a gift, Anna. I know how you adore your goddess." His gaze dropped to the torn dress and gashes in her skin. "I didn't expect you to hurt yourself during worship."

Anna looked down at the bared proof of her actions.

"Never do that again. I won't see you hurt." He pulled a handkerchief from his pocket, tucked it in her palm, and then gently pressed it to her wounds. Her limp grip held it there.

Pushing open her bedroom door, he led her inside and nudged it shut. He brushed his fingers across her cheek. "I've wanted you longer than life, it seems." He lightly kissed her lips and Anna leaned into his touch, closing her eyes. "I'd do anything to keep you safe. Keep you mine. Tell me you love me, Anna. Tell me the spells were unnecessary. That you wanted me all along."

"I love you. The spells were unnecessary. I wanted you all along."

Her keeper smiled. "Perhaps total compliance was uncalled for then." He pulled her close, the rumpled fabric of her bodice falling aside. Running his fingers through her hair, he looked deep into her eyes.

Her heart thumped and her breath hitched.

"You'll enjoy the life I offer. I can give you anything you desire." He nodded toward the hall. "I wanted the sanctuary to be a place for you to find peace. But it looks like I was mistaken."

His brows rose and Anna upped her own, basking in the loving expression. "Would you like an art studio? You could continue creating." He took her hands in his. "The hands of an artist, a creator of beauty." He held them to his chest and placed her thumbs and fingers together. "In more ways than one."

Anna's lips parted as she stared at the symbol created. Primal heat swirled in her core and faint promises floated just out of her understanding.

He looked at her sideways and cocked a grin. "The symbol arouses you, doesn't it, Anna? What does it mean? Did the wizards instill an added gift with the bid? They know, don't they? They have to, considering my requirements."

He brushed the lining from her shoulders and kissed along her collar. Shivers traveled down to her bosom. "I couldn't be happier. I couldn't find satisfaction in anything more."

The warm breath and light touch lifted her to float with the clouds. She wilted, head lulling to the side as a soft cry blew past his ear.

"You are the best thing I've ever afforded myself." He led his lips up to her neck. "The greatest prize I could have won."

Chapter Fourteen

Cole glared at the old mantle clock above the hearth. Just over twelve hours left to begin his ploy. Anticipation had long turned into vexation. The only thing worse than causing harm, was waiting for the right time to correct it.

The quiet study seemed irritatingly unbiased, as the second hand on the timer didn't even make a sound. He watched the tip slowly move around the circumference, eclipsing the tiny nocks one by one. Line. No line. Line. No line. Line. *No line.*

His exasperation exploded. Shooting his hand toward the thing, a statuette charged from the bookshelf and pierced the face of the timekeeper. He threw his disgruntled gaze to the door, immediately angry with himself for imitating Vincent's destructive temper.

"James!"

Wait. I bet he's still in bed. He glanced back at the clock to check the time and then scoffed at his stupidity. The damn thing was broke, its hands scrambled and bent, glass shattered with a miniature rendition of the Meridian capitol tower poking out at an odd angle. He dragged his hand across his chin and slumped in his master's chair.

"What are you doing up already?"

Cole's nerves jumped at the sudden voice. "I hate it when you do that."

James chuckled. "You called me."

"I didn't realize the time before I did." He motioned to the clock. "You wouldn't mind fixing that, would you?"

Stepping to the desk, James set a plate of cake down for him and another for himself. "Taking on Father Time?" He flicked his finger and the figurine returned to the bookshelf. Hands straightened and glass reassembled with tiny *clatters* and *clinks*.

He sat in a chair and forked at his snack. "Eat the cake. Elaina's family barely touched it. We have enough to last a year."

"Did you bring butter?"

"You want butter on a cake?"

"I'll eat butter on anything." He reached for his portion.

"No butter."

"How about sweet cream?"

"Just eat the cake."

Cole shoveled a bite into his mouth. "What are you doing up so early?"

James leaned his elbows on his knees. "Haven't been to bed. Well, I've been to bed. But my room's right under the—newlywed's suite."

"They're not married yet."

"Close enough. With her father's total acceptance the family promising sealed it."

Cole scoffed. "Eager to move up in the social ranks, wasn't he? I felt his every fiber shout yes when Mr. Ballard explained it."

"He does have a way of playing the cards. Well, he earns his pay."

"So they're still celebrating up there?"

"Wouldn't you be?" James grinned and eyed him. "You've been in here all night again, haven't you?"

"Can't sleep. Don't want to sleep." He sent a bitter look at James. "I don't need to relive what happened."

"If you don't get some rest you'll be a wreck by the time we get Anna here."

Cole smoothed his hands over his head and sighed. He knew his brother was right. He'd thought of little else; calculating, converging spells in theory, attempting to accomplish an acceptable outcome. Truth of the matter, every combination, spell or potion, promised a crippling or deadly outcome…except one. And that depended on what Anna had learned in her past lives. The procedure included such an array of interconnecting circumstances that even with his formidable knowledge of enchantment he was left with nothing but doubt.

He set his fork on the plate with a *clink* unable to stomach food. "Tell me she'll be okay, James."

"I wish I could, brother." He motioned to the Utopian. "I don't know if you've checked, but I looked into her past. It's filled with loss. Mother disappeared shortly after giving birth. Father was a street sweep. Impoverished, hopping from one shelter to another on Beggar's Row East. He passed away when she was seventeen. She managed to get a job with Cantrell a couple years ago as an artist."

Cole looked at him, a small grin lighting his lips. "An artist."

"She built a bit of a name for herself." James glanced at Cole. "Mostly through Dressen's favor of her work, it seems. Mr. Cantrell bragged about all the sales he made to him. Said he was a regular, requesting her as the artisan."

A scoff passed Cole's lips. "Gods, I hope she didn't decorate his foyer."

"She specialized in stained-glass."

He closed his eyes as he recalled the view of her at the mansion. "She was staring at that big stained-glass window." His comment drifted quietly as the innocence of her countenance sketched across his mind. "She seemed mesmerized by it. At peace." He let out a heavy breath and looked at James. "So you're telling me she's experienced hardship and loss up until Dressen started to take notice."

James nodded. "And now we plan to bring that all back to her."

"We're going beyond that, James. Memories of one lifetime are only a small portion of what comprises a soul." He ran his fingers across his weary brow. "If this lifetime brought her loss and pain, what about the others?"

Setting his plate on the desk, James clasped his hands. "These experiences may have made her strong. She obviously took a stand against Dressen's attentions. Her lifetimes may have ingrained self-preservation." He leaned his head to the side. "Either way, when she regains her memory, her will, and then we set free her ability to understand it all, she's going to go through a lot of pain. She'll relive her losses, at least from this life. It won't be easy."

Cole tossed his head to the side. Experiencing them through dreams was bad enough. But to force her to suffer through them in reality...

James seemed hesitant to say anything further. "Well, we'll be here for you. You have our support."

The comment should have imparted comfort but fell short in its intent. The supportive stand of his brothers meant more than Cole could relay with words and he wished James had developed the intuitive reading of emotions to help him out with this at times.

He nodded, attempting to push aside the thought of the procedure and look at the plan as a whole.

First things first. Get Anna out from under a Grand Marshal's keep.

Stained-glass that adorned Dressen's door like a headdress glowed softly as Cole led the way up the bobble-lit path. The spirit of celebration was underway as they entered. Several couples lingered in the large foyer, glasses of cordial in hand.

Elaina's emotions displayed pure awe and though Cole had only one purpose for being there he smiled to himself. Mianna's elation had been the same at her first high social. She was every bit as elegant as the Ladies of Nobility.

Then, carriages of silver and pearl pulled with high-stepping stallions delivered the elite to such functions and he was sure to prearrange the best for her delight. Her burgundy gown took over half the seating. His father mumbled under his breath at the tight quarters but Cole noticed the small glances he made in her direction. The senior Sentinel was pleased with her appearance and asked for her hand several times throughout the night in dance.

Cole understood his brother's desire to have his love attend. Elaina was every bit as beautiful in her own right. And Cole picked up the pride from Vincent at having her on his arm. It echoed Cole's own from the past.

Reg welcomed them in and helped Elaina remove her shawl.

Glancing around the grand foyer, Cole couldn't help notice the change in atmosphere. The gaudy crystals that draped the wall to the left illuminated the dimmed hall with soft light and reflected in the onyx pillars at its side. They created an enchanted atmosphere of welcome and delicate finery. The bronze hair lines on the opposing panel emitted a deep glow, revealing the form of a tree not noticeable under the usual bright glare of the domed ceiling.

Cole held up his hand as the manservant came to accept his wrap. "We'll keep ours." As the man left, he sent his thoughts to his brothers. *"I'll take care of things as quickly as possible and we'll leave."*

Vincent glanced at Elaina but nodded and followed him into the guest hall.

A graceful dance occupied the floor, moving to the strings of a mellow quartet. Every member of the Grand Marshal's court seemed in attendance accompanied by ladies of status.

Elaina held to Vincent's arm as he led her past several of the more gossipy gatherings. Gazes followed the couple. She was a stunning companion. The gown he'd gifted her clung to all the right curves and with her graceful movements no one would have guessed her a daughter of a lower class. Cole was pleased with the added attention on them. Fewer on his dealings.

He scanned the spacious hall. Laurel garland accented the caissons in the ceiling, symbolic of victory and position. Drapes of silver silk adorned the banisters of the second level, leaving trails of weaved fringe to sway in the breeze of the open terrace doors. Tri-paneled privacy screens stood at the sides of the musician's huddle. Lights glowed behind them, bringing to life the intricate stained-glass designs.

Anna's project.

Cole stifled a sneer and let his gaze wander among the guests. He accepted a cordial from a passing server and strolled along the circumference. Lords acknowledged him with nods or toasts of their drinks. Each echoed recognition of the Shilo City reapers. He knew every one of them—their taste in servers, their preference in control. He offered little in return for their greetings.

"Sir Cole." Dressen's baritone voice came from near the terrace doors before he'd caught sight of him.

"Lord Dressen." He smiled a complimentary greeting. "A pleasure to see you on this special occasion." He looked to Anna at his side.

She held his arm, fingers laced at the nook of his elbow. Her ivory satin gown fitted snugly. Smooth elegance flowed from the soft curve of her hips to the floor. As she turned to gaze upon her keeper, Cole noticed the design bared much of her back. Her hair swooped up into a loose herringbone weave, leaving wisps to trail her unveiled shoulders. Diamonds bejeweled her with a web of elegance and called attention to her favored position at the Lord's side.

A large hand lighted on Dressen's shoulder and Lord Standish leaned to his hearing. "Might I have a quick word?"

Stepping into a turn, Cole took a drink from his glass to allow privacy.

"Without the girl." The Grand Marshal motioned to Anna and then eyed Cole with a pardoning expression.

Lord Dressen remove Anna's hand from his arm. "Accompany Sir Shilo, Anna. I won't be long." He kissed her fingers and turned to his comrade.

Warmth flushed through Cole's heart as he turned back to his reason for being there. Anna. If it could only be that easy. A requested dance. A guide to the far end of the hall. A secluded passage and a whisk away by Smoke of Night. He'd have her—until Dressen found her missing after he'd entrusted her to him. He swallowed and tempered his desire, reminding himself of the plan.

Anna stepped to Cole and sent a questioning gaze along the length of his cape. He smiled and pulled aside his cloak to hold out his arm. She laced her hand around his elbow.

Exhilaration charged from their contact and he couldn't help but look into her eyes. How had he not recognized her call for what it was? So much could have been avoided if he had.

She looked up at him and hesitated as if studying his gaze. Her fingertips stroked her lips and Cole's heart skipped at the thought of her remembering their kiss. It was unlikely, but he picked up on feelings of—cherishment? He brushed his hand along hers to hold.

Gazing at his touch, she slowly reciprocated. It was true. Her cheeks flushed. Out of instinct? His soul willed it to be more.

His attention was pulled to the escalating conversation behind them.

Dressen's deep voice could only hush to a rumble. "They can't hurt us."

"There are ancient ways."

Cole widened his perception and picked up on variations of their emotions. Concern. Denial. Fear? Passiveness. Then with a hissed attempt at quiet, he heard the overlord's exhortation. "Carlton, you read too many tales to your children. Relax. I know what I'm doing."

Carlton huffed and his anger flew through Cole's senses. "What you're dealing with goes beyond mortal understanding, Kyle. We're not talking about common laws here."

"Look." There was no restraint in his voice this time as Dressen spoke. "Traditionalism has no place in this society and I weary of your constant hindrance. If you and your comrades want to levy another stand, by all means try. Your orthodox positions will not sway the counsel. I hold the majority in my pocket. Whatever you're little crusade comes up with will be overruled three to one. Now stop wasting my time. I have other interests to attend to."

Dressen stepped to their side. "Please excuse the intrusion." He smiled. "Differing opinions are prevalent in my line of duty."

"Indeed."

He took Anna's hand and set it on his arm. "Now, I've been anxiously awaiting your arrival, Sir Cole. Not all receive a gift forged by one such as you."

Cole motioned to the terrace. "This gift is best received in private." He glanced at Anna. "Of course, your lovely lady may accompany us."

Dressen eyed him sideways. "Why in private?"

"The elements may bring about an elated emotion." He smiled. "Exhilaration is not always something we want others to witness."

The Lord chuckled and Cole felt the man's anticipation heighten. "The terrace it is."

They stepped out into the crisp night air and Cole closed the doors behind him. The rumble of conversation and music hushed.

A soft breeze blew across the landing, rustling the ferns that bordered the cobblestoned patio. Bobbles beneath the foliage dimmed and brightened with the disturbance.

He stepped to the center of the terrace and withdrew the small copper box from his pocket. The trinket glowed, crystal at its center pulsed.

"This box holds a gift only you can control. I will present you with a small portion of its possibilities. I do this to reassure you if you have any hesitance in acquiring it."

Eager acceptance echoed from Dressen and his eyes gleamed. Cole slowly tilted the lid back. The lavender cloud inside flowed with the disturbance. He pinched at the substance and it lifted with his touch, a sleek trail following his motion. "With your permission, I present you with memories of your first birthday."

Humor puffed with Dressen's breath. "Who remembers their first birthday?"

"You." Cole nodded to urge the sire to open his hand. With a graceful wave, he led the essence to settle into the outstretched palm. The mist swirled. Violet overtook lilac as it solidified into a lustrous pearl. Folding the lord's hand into a fist, he gently placed his fingertips on the sire's eyes lids to close them. He muttered his command. *"Merota."*

Lord Dressen's brows rose. A quiet sound passed his lips and he shook his head. "Amazing. It's our birthday. Some of our old photographs were taken inside, but this was on the terrace and the blue lights are dimmed. I don't remember my parents mentioning blue lights...but...this is definitely me. I can feel it." Unmistakable astonishment rode his sigh. "There was a magician. He made things dance—sand? My, he was good. Where's Kayla?" He seemed to search with his closed eyes. "She had to have loved this."

Cole watched as Dressen's attention deepened on the memory.

"Mother probably hid her from that reporter they say got past security. Every newscaster in the area wanted the story. It was quite the event." The birthday boy shook his head. "What is that scent? Coconut? No. Almond. The treats taste so sweet." He raked his teeth over his bottom lip with a chuckled. "I think my father ate too much of them. I can smell it all over him. Anise?"

His lids lifted with his enthusiasm and then his heavy brows dipped. "Where did it go? It's gone."

"It's easiest to focus with closed eyes. Within this moment you just recalled, every detail was exact in its presentation to your mind and senses. Now, with this experience, you see the possibilities this gift can offer. I have enhanced these memories for your delight. You may remember any period of time in your life. Whether it's a forgotten occurrence during a court meeting or simply a past pleasure, it may be called upon at your leisure by holding the pearl and pinpointing the occurrence in your mind."

He lowered the box, careful not to close the lid. "With this gift, I'm compelled to issue a warning."

"A warning. What could possibly cause need of a warning with a gift like this?"

"Some experiences, as you well know, arouse deeper pleasures. With the enhancement I placed on the gift, you may find it difficult to call yourself out of the memory. Reliving passions can become intoxicating in the intensified state. It's up to you to call an end to it."

Dressen's crooked smile confirmed Cole's expectations. *Very pleased with the gift.*

"So, I can call up any memory, any moment, and relive it in detail as it happened—in a heightened state."

"That's right."

The lord laughed and shook his head. "I never expected such an extraordinary gift, Sir Cole. In all my life, I would have never imagined." He lifted the little pearl between his forefinger and thumb. "If you don't mind, I think I'd like to test the extent of this little gem."

Clutching the lavender enchantment with his fist, he eased into a lounge chair.

Cole cocked a grin. "I thought you might."

As Dressen relaxed into a dream-like state, Cole turned his attention to Anna. She watched the lord with serene patience. He lifted the box and whispered to her mind. *"Anna."*

As she looked his way, he fanned his fingers. Light ginger clouded her eyes. *"Visola comp."*

She blinked with a start and shook head. Recognition flashed on her face. With the spell of vague recollection set in her mind, Cole shot an urgent thought to her. *"Curfew, run!"*

She gasped and then darted from the terrace toward town. Cole turned and flew open the ballroom doors. Music from the celebration spilled into the air. He marched inside, scanning the throng. Finding James and Vincent on the dance floor, he called to their minds. *"It is complete."*

Vincent halted his dance with Elaina and took her hand. She nodded and together they turned toward the exit. James bowed to his partner and as he joined Vincent, Cole set a long stride across the hall to the door. Their cloaks reefed with simultaneous motion as their heels hammered across the marble floor in cadence.

Conversations quieted and the guests quickly shuffled aside. Astonishment and wonder resounded around the ballroom and flooded Cole's senses. He led the way to the foyer and tossed a mental command at the doors. The large double entry flew wide.

Vincent raised his hand and Elaina's shawl zipped into his grasp from the coatroom. Crossing the threshold, he took her waist and pulled her tightly to him.

Cole barely noticed his brothers' cloaks furl as he whipped his own high and took on the Smoke of Night.

Chapter Fifteen

Anna ran, a single thought ebbing, resurfacing, distorting. *Curfew breakers are never heard from again.*

Abstract symbols flashed before her mind's eye, a multitude of color. Panic.

The dim lights of the silent city jeered at her with each flicker as she hastened through its empty streets. A tall palisade. Familiar. Gone.

She halted and looked down the fortification. Recollection. Hope was beyond. She darted, searching for a break in the barrier. Not until she came to a crossroads, did she pause. A gateway, hulking in size. She gazed, mollified at the mortared arch on the corner of—*Simpson Drive? Arbital Street?* The large stone griffin glared down at her with granite eyes. *A guardian? An obstructer?*

She blinked and shook her head at the scenes in her mind. *The gates were closed.* She threw her gaze to them. Open. *Misted pavement.* She looked down the street. The memory was gone.

Crossing the threshold, a dark wonderland of incense filled the air—roses, lilacs, lilies. *Follow the path.* Faint recollection guided her feet. A bridge. *Cross the bridge.*

Mists undulated as she stepped beyond the pass-over and immediately confusion haunted her mind. She cried a desperate weep and gazed wildly around the dense shadows that engulfed the grounds. She pounded her head with her fists. Confusion. She broke into a run. Racing through the low fog, she flailed her arms about her, trying to ward off the provoking cover. It slowly reverted, mocking her hasty opposition.

The trail ended and she halted again. She panted with uncertainty. A small one-lane road. Row houses hosted narrow frontages. Care-worn automobiles hugged the curb like a crutch, standing wearily, partially on the pavement.

She scanned the compacted neighborhood. Flashes of laughter, hospitality, and common ground lighted her mind. She followed the feeling of placement. *Left? No right.* She walked.

Half way down the hole-pocked street, a sunken doorway caught her attention. Meager bushes graced each side and a wind chime tinkled in the small breeze. Her heart grasped the word *home.*

She dashed to the entrance and tugged at the rusty latch. Locked. Fright gripped her. "Let me in!"

Scrambling behind a bush to peer into the paned window, she pressed her cheek against the barrier and looked around. A kitchen, a bar, yellow wallpaper, and a closet. "This is my house." She dug her fingernails into the wooden frame. Weathered sealant pierced the tender skin under her nails and chunks fell to the sill, adding to the peeled brown paint. "My home!"

Panels lurched against the loose molds as she drummed on the panes. Focusing solely on the interior's promise of reprieve, she pounded harder. Glass shattered and fretted wood splintered, leaving jagged spears protruding from the casing. Entry was a climb away.

She grasped the framework and pulled herself onto the ledge. Anything she could grab served as support and leverage as she scrambled through the opening.

Ivory satin ripped. Her bare arms raked against the broken wood. Heaving herself over the frame, she dragged her body across the shard glass. Piercing pain dug deep into her hips and thighs and she gasped as she tumbled into the kitchen. Blood flowed down the yellow wall below the window. Her hands slipped on the linoleum as she threw her arms out to catch herself. Clambering for the bar, she braced her stand. Pain gripped her lower body but confusion overruled any thought of reason.

"Anna."

Her lids shot wide. Who spoke her name? She whipped around so fast nausea rushed her. The little kitchen blurred as her gaze flitted to each surface. With a quick swipe, she wiped the sweat from her face and looked beyond the bar to the small living area. The haze lifted.

A phone sat on the sofa table. She scampered around the narrow divider and dove for the receiver. Her fingers groped it tight as she cried into the mouthpiece. "Please, help me, somebody *please* help me!"

A dark mist appeared in her peripheral and she caught her breath, inching her gaze toward the entrance. It filtered through the crack beneath the door and then billowed into the form of two men.

She froze.

Something deep inside told her there should be three. The thought disappeard. As the tall slender one's gaze swept up her body, her heart skipped. She knew him. Somewhere in her mind, she knew him and couldn't tear her gaze away from his midnight irises.

"Oh, Gods, Anna."

The slight tone in his whisper sent goose bumps up her arms and as he slipped the receiver from her loosened grip, all she wanted was to take the fright from his voice. The trance turned to shock as he grabbed the shredded portions of her gown and ripped the fabric aside. A sick growl sounded in his throat.

His large companion quickly waved his hand and tiny spars of glass flew from her wounds. A shriek squelched in her gasp as nettles jetted across her body.

Dropping to his knee, the man before her gently covered a large gash in her hip with his palm. Heat pooled around the cut. When he removed his hand, the wound was gone. He passed the healing power over the intrusions in her thighs. Pain subsided and Anna closed her eyes, savoring the comfort.

Heaving a sigh, the tall man brushed his fingers over the smaller tracks up her arms and along her side. She looked down at his long black hair as his feather touch traveled the back of her legs.

Weariness swam alongside wonderment in her mind. Placing her hands on the crown of his head, she pulled him close to her torso.

He paused, buried his face in her skin. His hands gently skimmed up her hips and then held her waist. Hot breath bathed her abdomen and sent chills through her core. She licked her dry lips and closed her eyes.

Cole savored the scent of Anna's body, holding her close as his heavy breath bathed her skin. Sweet musk from her wakening senses filled him with a longing from ages past. He brushed his lips down her abdomen and drank in the intoxicating aroma.

She wavered and her hands became heavy on his head. A thought raced to the forefront, *too much blood loss, no one could survive.*

James' voice called him from his reverie. "Cole."

He lifted his gaze to her and shot to a stand. Her limp body fell into his embrace. He gathered her into his arms. She was ghostly pale and fear shot through him. "She's lost too much blood."

"Get her back to the manor, I'll clean up here."

With a swoop of his cloak, he relinquished their forms and darted out the window into the night. Through the cold midnight travel, his panicked thoughts sent prayers to the gods of Cornerstone Deep.

"Arylin, Goddess of Love, grant me this my prayer. Take not again my love from me. Gryffin, Protector of Conformance, forgive my ignorance. Preserve the guiltless in mine arms. Taravaughn, Giver of Beauty and Life, restore that which was taken through despair."

He'd never prayed to them and his hope was weak as to their acknowledging his plea. But his heart cried to every possibility. Her actions tore at his conscience and he pushed harder to quicken their arrival.

His dark mass threw open the cherry wood manor door. He ignored Elaina's gasp and flew up the marble-capped stairs. Vincent dashed after him and she quickly followed.

Entering a guestroom, Cole took form and gently lowered Anna onto the bed. Brushing the disheveled hair from her face, he sat at her side. The dim light from the hall bathed them in solemn silence. *Gods, what have I done?*

He heaved a deep breath and looked away. An apricot tree brushed against the window as if the blossoms were trying to decide the fate of his love. The large wardrobe loomed in the shadow, quietly rebuking the sight. The mirror atop the wide dresser reflected their subdued forms against the glow from the entrance. Seeing his distraught face sickened him, deepening his anxiety.

Vincent and Elaina rushed to his side.

Elaina's face paled as she scanned Anna, dress torn and blood stained. "Cole, what happened? Who is she?"

Vincent waved his hand and the room lit. "It's Anna."

"Who?"

Cole glanced at her, realizing she'd never met her father's employee. "She's been hurt badly. Lost a lot of blood."

"I'll get the things to clean her up." She rushed from the room.

"And water," Vincent called after her. "She'll need water. And a warm blanket."

Returning his gaze to the pallid visage of his love, Cole shook his head. "I can heal wounds but I can't restore what's been lost." His heart ached, thickening his chest, and made it difficult to breathe. He swallowed hard and his eyes stung as tears forced their way under his lids. "Kid, you should have seen the place. There was blood everywhere. The doors, the floor..."

Shock flowing from his brother only intensified Cole's anguish. He knew Vincent was at a loss for words. He doubted any attempt to comfort or reassure would help quell his fears anyway.

Closing his eyes, tears seeped past his lashes, freeing the emotions that brimmed in his heart. He rested his head on her bosom and took her into his arms. Then succumbing to grief, he wept.

Cole kept a steady watch on Anna's colorless face. He barely breathed as his empty lungs refused further relief.

A soft tap came at the door and Elaina tilted her head, compassion vivid in her countenance and the emotions flowing from her. She set a tray with a pitcher of water, a cup, and cleaning material on the bed stand and then repositioned the thick comforter in her arms.

Cole sighed and reluctantly stood. Elaina placed the blanket at the foot of the bed and sat at Anna's side. Feeling displaced, Cole tugged a corner wingchair near and sank into the cushions. He stretched his longs legs in front of him and rested his forehead on his hand.

More monotonous ticks filled the room as Elaina sponged Anna's body clean. He peeked through the tops of his lids as she stood and withdrew a gown from the folds of the comforter. She glanced at him and he lowered his gaze. Nothing would make him leave Anna's side, modesty-minded nursemaid or not.

Elaina tucked a heavy comforter around Anna with the care of nestling a baby in a crib. "I'll get more water, Cole, but she really needs a hospital."

He kneaded his tightened brow with his fingers. "They can't know she's up here."

"I could take her in. They don't need to know she's staying here."

"You don't understand the situation, Elaina." He sighed at having to explain. "Where's Vincent?"

She motioned to the door. "In the study, talking with James."

He glanced at her, sending a disgruntled gaze her way. "He needs to be talking with you. It's his place to calm his woman's fretting."

She flushed red and blinked at him. Turning for the door, she quickly left.

Cole released a breath of frustration and dragged his hand over his face, knowing how harsh he'd sounded. He had enough to deal with and another woman's concern was the last thing he needed.

With all his efforts focused on freeing Anna, he never stopped to think that she would panic in such a way. Her deep wounds and pools of blood showed bright against his eyelids every time he closed them. Regret deepened each time he rested his eyes.

Exhaustion washed over him with nauseating force and he took a deep breath to waken his fatigued mind. He felt James' concern and he glanced to the door.

"How's she doing?"

Cole shook his head and didn't bother hiding the resignation in his voice. "James, how was I supposed to know she'd dive through a window to get to something familiar? I only touched on her memories to make her recall the need to run."

James stepped into the room and leaned on the wall. "Don't beat yourself up. You couldn't have known."

"Blood was everywhere."

"I took care of that. Nobody will be able to tell anything happened."

That wasn't what he meant. But by the compassion emitting from his brother he realized James was only attempting to fill the void. How could anyone know what to say to make things right? For that matter, how could anyone make things right? There was a strong possibility Anna wouldn't pull out of this. He knew it and he knew his brothers knew it.

Cole shifted in his seat as the thought ate at his gut. In her case, if her life ended so did her soul's progression. Completely. "She can't die, James." He swallowed hard. "Not now."

James sighed and looked at the vial in his hand. "I can't gather lost blood. Purity is compromised when I do. But, I think I might be able to help with the production."

Cole peeked through the miniscule opening between his lids. "You can't duplicate a person's blood."

"I'm not talking about copying blood and conducting a transfusion." He held out the small container. "I haven't told anyone, but I did an essence trace on Sarah."

Cole looked at him. Of course, he knew this.

James pursed his lips. "She's very ill. I thought at first it had to do with an inability to produce sufficient blood. So, I've been working on a potion to accelerate its production."

A chill swept Cole's heart and he lifted his head, realizing what his brother's words meant.

"Her name is Tiffiny now." James smiled a little. "But she has a disease that's far too advanced to correct. She doesn't have long to live."

Cole held his anticipation, waiting for the right moment. "I'm sorry, James."

James nodded. "It should work on Anna."

As he grasped the small bottle, unmitigated relief flooded Cole's soul.

"She needs to drink it. Even if it's a little at a time, see that she swallows it all. And pray."

A hush fell over Cole's face. "I've already done that."

James set his large hand on his shoulder. "As have I."

Chapter Sixteen

Vincent pulled Elaina into a tight embrace and stroked her strawberry hair. Warmth seeped through his shirt as her tears dampened his shoulder. His heart tugged at his chest. He tilted his head to peer at her watery face. "Don't cry. I told you Cole was moody. Don't let him get to you."

"Vince, you didn't hear him." A sob punctuated her words. "I was only trying to help. I don't understand why he doesn't just—wave a hand or something and make her better."

"Elaina." He leaned back to gaze into her eyes. "Sometimes we can manipulate flesh to heal, but we don't have power over life. We're not gods."

She wrinkled her brow. "Vince, if your magic keeps you alive for so long, how can it not keep her alive?"

A small smile touched his lips. "Our magic doesn't prolong our lives. Our nature does. It's how we were created." He brushed his fingers down her cheek. "Your gods chose a shorter life-cycle for their children." His grin inched up his cheek. "Some say we have long lives because it takes that long to get anything to sink into our thick skulls."

Instead of the joke lightening the mood, another serious topic rolled from her tongue.

"*Our* gods? We don't have the same gods?"

"Each realm is distinct in their creation. Each has its set of gods."

Elaina paled as quickly as she flushed and her gaze shifted to the tapestries that hung beside the hearth. Meridian's blue sun sank below fields of amber and white weeping woodlands woven within the threads. No doubt a myriad of questions ran through her mind. Viewing the difference between the most ancient, distant realm in the depictions must conjure all sorts of alter-realities.

He nodded and stepped beside the artwork, taking the opportunity to get her mind off Cole's rash behavior. Motioning to the image on the third wall-hanging, he lifted his brows in fondness. "This is Meridian, my home. It's the oldest dimension in the Arched Spectrum of Realms. You might call it the mother of the planes. She's the original that all others are patterned after." He glanced at her with a wink. "I tried to explain that to you in the park. One day, the other realms may progress to the point we are now. But they have many millennia to go before that can happen."

She gnawed on her lip with a little grin. "But we don't have a blue sun or five moons."

"No. Terra's a cornerstone dimension and has a yellow one. Midway dimensions have white." A breath of humor puffed from his nostrils. "Don't ask me why. But it's symbolic somehow."

"Progressive intensity?"

"Hm. Perhaps. And the five moons are reflections of the other dimensions' moons...aside from our own. Many think of them as a crown. All other planes see one." He shrugged.

"Who are your gods, Vince?"

Reverenced by the thought, he looked at the crystal globes that sat at the center of the bookshelf behind Cole's desk. Stepping to them, he placed his hand on the left sphere. "This crystal was given to my mother and father when Cole was born. It was a gift from Aditi, God of Creation." He brushed his fingers across the next in line. "This one was given fifty years later when James was born. A gift from Dyas, God of Knowledge. And this one," he picked up the last and it glowed at his touch. "Was given to them three hundred years after that, when I was born. It's from Iradal, God of Life."

His voice hushed as he gazed into the token. "It's not often a Meridian couple is blessed with three children. Long life spans hinder re-incarnation somewhat. The fact that Aditi presented a Triad crystal to my parents when Cole was born signified they were chosen. They knew Iradal would intervene and birth a new soul, if needed."

Honor filled him. "This is my first life cycle."

"Your first... You mean James and Cole have lived before? Re-incarnation really exists?"

Glancing back to her, he realized he'd offered much more information than he intended. He set the crystal back on its plinth and turned to her. "Rebirth exists throughout the realms, Elaina. It's how our souls progress, learn. Cole and James are both living in their third lifetime."

Placing his hands on Elaina's shoulders, Vincent gazed into her blue eyes. "Anna is Cole's last wife, Elaina. Her name was Mianna and she is his soul mate. He's been lost since her death nearly four hundred years ago. He just found her again in Anna and nothing's going to keep him from doing everything in his power to save her. You need to trust him."

Elaina's wide gaze searched his and as she flexed her wrist, he knew the promise band told her of the truthfulness of his statement. A slow nod lifted her chin as she pulled him close and rested her head on his collar.

"Wow," she breathed. "I could have never imagined this. But it's like I've always known." She wrapped her arms around his waist and bunched his shirt in her fists. "Oh, Vince, I'm so proud to be part of your family. I'll help anyway I can. I promise I'll be right here."

"I know." He held her in a tight embrace. "Right now just comfort her. Much more happened than what you see. She's very confused. And when the time comes for us to undo the harm your support will be very important."

Her gaze met his and her words came without hesitation. "I'll be there, Vince."

Elaina's love flowed through every vein in Vincent's body and for the first time, he realized what it meant. Her soul called to his, penetrated his being and bound him to her like none ever had or would again. Eternity stretched before him, filled with Elaina's love.

Vincent flushed with understanding. *Cole experiences this when he looks at Anna. Gods, the pain he must be going through at what happened.*

He set his jaw as determination swelled in his heart. Whatever it took, he'd be there to support his brother through what he knew would be the most difficult process ever undertaken.

Chapter Seventeen

Cole unstopped the slender vial and gently lifted Anna's head to administer the potion. As he carefully tipped the container to her lips, tremors traveled down his forearms. His hands quaked. The amber liquid jumped to the brim and he quickly tilted it upright. *Gods, Cole, control yourself. She needs every drop.*

A soft palm rested on his wrist and Cole's gaze shot to Elaina's. When had she returned and how did he not pick up on the strong compassion emitting from her when she had? Her blue eyes looked deep into his, understanding with a touch of sadness. "Let me do that, Cole. You've been through enough."

He wasn't sure if the tremors were from anticipating a fortunate outcome or from sheer anxiety over the whole ordeal, but he accepted her tender attention as a blessing. Vincent's intervention with her was evident. He watched as she patiently poured small measures into Anna's mouth.

Elaina turned to Cole and lifted the emptied container. "Well, that's it. She got it all."

He sighed. "Thank you."

"Anything, Cole." She smiled and set the vial on the bed stand. "What about you? Can I get you a drink? It might calm you some."

Nodding, he offered a small smile.

"Good, then. I'll be right back."

As she closed the door behind her, Cole eased himself onto the bed. "Don't give up, Anna." His faint words were swallowed by the silence of the room. "I'll fix this and see to it nothing ever happens to you again." Brushing his fingertips over her hair, he solemnly whispered a plea. "Don't leave me."

Her soft locks sent countless memories rushing through his mind. Her smile, her cheeky comments, her blue eyes dancing as if life itself was a game. Her Arylinite spirit embraced every moment of love, able to see beneath façades that others deemed as truth. He sighed, knowing that side of her may have been unique to that lifetime—a result of her specialized upbringing in the Arylin colony of the northern territory.

He tilted his head and gazed over her still face. Her features were remarkably similar to Mianna's. The gentle slope of her nose, the way she chose to wear her dark hair long, and he couldn't deny her blue eyes when she'd looked at him. He cupped her cheek with his hand, gently stroking her lips with his thumb. They curved from a bow-tie center into a natural smile. So soft. Inviting. He leaned to her and lightly kissed them, then leaned his cheek to hers.

"Talk to me, Anna." His breath was a plea. As much as he knew no answer would come, his heart called to her with his deepest wish.

He brushed his fingers down her neck to her chest, tenderly caressing her pale skin at the neckline of her gown. A strained pause caught his throat as he lightly followed her breast to her ribcage. "What's in your heart?"

The tiny circles he drew on the thin fabric fed his longing for her touch. Supple creases followed his motion. To have her arms around him, the love they brought, had given him unmitigated comfort in a past life. It could be so again.

"My life was yours." He kissed the circles he created. "Every moment, I found joy in you."

He looked at her closed eyes. "Please, don't leave me. Please promise you'll be mine again."

No emotion showed upon the visage of his love, but distant echoes of vows lighted his soul.

"Open to me." He wondered if his whispered thought could possibly reach her unconscious mind. *"Speak to me with your soul."*

Her lips parted and a chill flew through him. He waited, listened intently. Weak sensations touched his senses. "Anna," he said aloud, hope rising. He cupped his palm to her cheek again. "Fight for it. Call to me."

Anna remained silent.

Cole's heart ached. Yet, that small reaction spurred his resolve. He framed her face as he lowered to take her lips with his. "I'll help you."

The scent of licorice and cream fell from his lips as he called on his Breath of Zephyr . His soul's voice owned his words. "My life is a mirage of endless time. But you engulf me, rivet my mind, encompass my soul."

She inhaled his sensual gift and gasped for deeper intake.

Yes. Hope impossibly filled him. His muscles tightened with expectation. His heart pounded against his chest. *"Call to me!"*

Quick taps sounded from the door and Elaina opened it a crack. "Cole, um, Lord Dressen is here to see you. And," she glanced down the hall, "he has others with him. They refused the parlor. They wanted to wait in the foyer. They don't look happy."

Cole released his breath and clenched his teeth, quickly looking over the quiet face of his love. He sighed. *Of all times for interruption.*

He glanced at the clock on the bed stand. Five o'clock a.m. He figured he'd be contacted at some point, but this was sooner than expected. "Stay with her, Elaina. I'll take care of this."

Cole kept his stride steady as he descended the staircase. James and Vincent stood beside the banister Sentinel to his left. Dressen mumbled to his comrades in the center of the hall. Five accompanied the lord, each a highly ranked Grand Marshal. Elaina was right. They weren't happy. A strong sense of ill-affect echoed from the group.

Curving his lips into a congenial smile, he walked to them. "Lord Dressen, I trust your celebration was a success."

Dressen turned without pleasantries and stated his purpose. "Where is she?"

"Excuse me?"

"You know damn well what I said. Where is she?"

Taking a deep breath, Cole leaned his head toward the lawmaker. "I can only assume you're speaking of the young woman you escorted to the event."

"You were the last to see her, Sir Shilo. The guests told me the three of you left directly after you entered from the terrace."

Cole glanced at the gathering, several of whom he recognized as guests in the ballroom when they exited. "And I'm sure they also informed you that we left alone. I wasn't aware you put her in my care while you explored the extents of the gift."

Dressen growled. "I didn't."

"Then why would you think I would know of her absence?"

The lord huffed and looked away. "Well, she's nowhere to be found."

"I'm certain she merely wandered onto the grounds."

"We've checked the grounds! We've checked everywhere." His gray gaze carried a commanding glare as he looked into Cole's eyes. "I want her found and returned to me by midnight tonight."

Cole raised his brows. "A re-harvesting?"

"Call it what you like, my bid will be filled."

He shifted his stand and clasped his hands, lifting his chin. "I must say, Lord Dressen, this is unusual. Once a bid is satisfied, the trade is complete."

Dressen's features went livid. "If I find any cause to suspect your involvement in her disappearance, I'll have the entire court of Grand Marshals on your backs! This order was bid in faith of an honest transaction."

A sizzle ran the length of Cole's spine as the circumstances surrounding Anna's harvest tainted the words. "Indeed."

"By tonight, Sir Shilo." The lord turned and marched out the front door. Several gazes sent judgment Cole's way before the group followed.

As the door slammed, he looked at his brothers. "That was quick. It seems I overestimated his love of the gift."

James cocked an eyebrow and set his hands on his waist. "At least we got her here. He can't prove anything unless they search the house."

Vincent huffed. "And that's not happening. They have no authority here."

"Cole."

Elaina's voice cut through the conversation and pulled Cole's attention to the top of the stairs. "What is it? Is something wrong?"

"She's awake." Elaina motioned down the hall. "And she's scared. Cole, she asking for her Keeper."

Heavenly relief flooded Cole's being and he darted up the steps, down the hall, and through Anna's bedroom door. Her gaze snapped to him and didn't vary as he slowed his approach and sat at her side. "Anna? Are you okay?"

Confusion, fear, comfort, and then confusion again resounded through him as her emotions touched his. He brushed his fingers across her cheek and looked deep into her blue eyes as he reclaimed his position. "Anna, I am your Keeper. Don't be afraid."

Her chest heaved a heavy sigh and she drew her hands from the thick layer of covers. Wrapping her arms around him, she pulled him close. Warmth flooded him as her instant contentment touched his soul. Sweet hope swelled in his chest. He had her in his arms and nothing would keep him from correcting this wrong.

Chapter Eighteen

James couldn't help notice the woman's shapely figure as the gathered skirt flared at her hips and the bodice was filled with bosom. She stood there, staring at him on the threshold of Shilo Manor. A black band held her blonde hair away from her forehead and the purple cardigan she wore clashed dramatically with the lemonade yellow sundress beneath it. She twisted her fingers together calling attention to her bleach-clean nails.

It must be important. Most fail to remember why they came this way, thanks to the charm cast to protect them from the curious. To appear on their doorstep proved her determination. She blinked her teary blue eyes.

A soft breeze blew across the porch and she opened her lush mouth. He upped his brow in expectation. She closed it again.

He lifted his hand in question. "Is there something you wanted, ma'am?"

She blinked with a start and then laughed a breath. "I was just—I mean...wow. Elaina was right."

"Excuse me?"

She waved a sleeve-covered hand. "I thought *Vince* was something but look at *you*. All three of you must just be—magic made flesh."

What? He unconsciously stepped back, gazing over her cocked grin, full nose, heavy lidded eyes, and then her rounded chin. Shaking himself mentally, he forced a cool demeanor. "And you are?"

"Oh, I'm Linda. Elaina's sister."

Another blow of unexpected information. Heat rushed up his neck. Then, he recalled... Vincent had mentioned a sister from out of town attended the family's gathering. Why hadn't he included her when they presented the family with promise bands? What were the odds that Elaina had spoken of things with her sibling around? Mighty high in light of the comments the woman had just made.

James forced a congenial smile. "You didn't join your family when they accepted our invitation the other day."

"Yeah, well, I tried to talk my husband into it." She glanced to the side, obviously uneasy with the subject. "It's kind of why I'm here to see her."

"Your husband?" *Dear, Gods. More possible repercussions.* James opened the door further, urgency gripping his nerves. "Please, come in."

As she crossed the threshold, he headed for the parlor. "Elaina's upstairs. I'll get her while you wait in the parlor."

He glanced back and motioned toward the room. She quickened her steps, wiping her face with her elongated sleeves, and then pulled the band from her hair. She fluffed her locks. "Thank you. You have a lovely place here."

Opening the parlor door, he paused as the bar came to view. Under normal circumstances, he'd offer a lady a drink. But as it was, all he wanted to do was call on Vincent and his betrothed. Heaving a breath to calm his nerves, he decided on chivalry. He smiled at her as she settled into the sofa. "May I offer you a drink?"

"Yes, thank you."

How much had Elaina shared of their nature? Had Linda spoken to her husband of the news? Had he spread it further? As the amber liquid poured, he had to glance at her.

Pink tinged her cheeks and she lowered her gaze.

He replaced the flask.

"You know, I thought you'd look more like Vince. But..."

Caught once again by her words, James turned and looked at her. She upped her brows and her shoulders lifted. He glanced down at his appearance, momentarily distracted from his concerns. No stains on his vested chest. Plenty of room in his sleeves for his bulky arms. Cuffs were a bit tight, but styled for the season. Trousers sufficiently creased, and he was sure his hair was kempt.

He gazed at her and had to ask. "But?"

She breathed a laugh. "You're just..." she motioned an encompassing circle. "Bigger. I mean, larger. Oh, good Gryffin." She covered her eyes with a hand that didn't hide the deep rosy color that bloomed on her face. "I'm so sorry! You're gorgeous."

Heat swept across his cheeks and he handed her the cordial. "Well, thank you. I'll go get Elaina."

"Yes." She accepted the glass and shook her head, looking away. "That's a good idea."

As he left the room, her whisper carried through the air. "For the love of Gryffin, Linda. Could you have made a worse impression?"

James tilted his head and trotted up the stairs. Reason hoped for a simple fix but his gut told him otherwise.

❦

Cole flexed his fingers around the crystal vase as he headed down the hall. Excitement bubbled at the threshold of a blossoming relationship with Anna more than with any woman he'd pursued since Mianna. Even though logic told him her true identity would be hidden, he couldn't harness his anticipation. Instincts revealed a shadow of her personality and that was enough to start. Whoever she'd grown to be since that sweet daughter of the Arylin colony would be the flower of his soul.

Noonday sunrays poured through the window and filled her guestroom with warmth. His heart wrapped around the serene scene and he smiled. Setting the roses on the corner table, he glanced around. The room was empty. "Anna?"

"Yes?"

He cautiously stepped to the bathroom and peered inside the open door. Her gaze locked on him and he flushed. Her gown lay at her feet and she held a folded towel on her lap as she sat on the bench in front of the vanity. "Are you okay?"

"Where's Clair?"

Cole glanced to the side, trying to remember the name. *Ah, Dressen's assigned aide.* He looked back at her and consciously made an effort to keep his gaze from wandering her unveiled body. "Clair's not here."

She looked at the marble tub. "Clair told me not to run a bath. She's supposed to help me."

"I see." Stepping into the small room, he pulled the curtain to the bathing area aside. "You can take a shower. It won't flood the room."

He turned the faucet on and selected a comfortable temperature. "Just—take a shower instead—of a bath. Er, just don't stop the drain as for a bath."

He cringed at his poorly executed statement, but his nerves danced at her exposure.

She stood and set the towel on the vanity. He averted his gaze but his peripheral vision betrayed his chivalrous intent. Heat flushed his skin. Muscles tightened. He swallowed his breath to control the affects.

He hadn't expected this. Perhaps a sleepy awakening, a presenting of flowers, mild conversation, but not this...

She gingerly stepped inside and Cole pulled the curtain home behind her.

Heaving a sigh, he closed his eyes. *Gods!* His attraction to her was too strong to begin their acquaintance in the nude. *Just leave, Cole. It's best just to...*

She pulled the curtain aside and his gaze snapped to the unexpected action. Water streamed from her drenched hair, sending floods to veer from her breasts and flow within the cleavage and down her slender belly.

His flush deepened and he forced his gaze upward. Sprinkles of water sparkled on her cheeks and beaded on her lashes. His voice cracked. "I—is something wrong?"

"If Clair isn't here to help me bathe, are you?"

His stomach knotted. "You want me to help you bathe?"

"She said I did it wrong."

A quick breath passed his lips as the urge to join her flew through him. *Calm down. Think rationally.* Chivalry reminded him it could lead to something he would regret, but desire goaded him. He caved, allowing his gaze to float down her petite form.

Wrong thing to do. Anticipation pooled in his stomach and lower.

Glancing away, he considered the options. *It's only a few minutes in a shower*, he reasoned, *to aide in a bath. Nothing more.* The weight of her gaze, innocent, unyielding, pressed him to decide.

Don't look down. Agreeing with his thoughts, he anchored his gaze on her cherubic face. *Again, wrong thing to do.* The pull that had called to him in the alley nearly overpowered him. He wanted to kiss those bow-tie lips, relive the blissful moment, answer her soul's call.

Clenching his teeth, he focused on the waterfall above her head. He inched the lever to lighten the flow and smiled. "Better?"

She turned and her shoulder brushed his chest, dampening his shirt with warmth. A spark flew from her touch to his core. Temptation reared and his gaze succumbed, lowering to view her bare back; the gentle slope of her waist, the slight V at the crown of her buttocks.

Cole's mind reeled. His manhood throbbed. Knees weakened and he grasped the shower curtain just because it was there. He wanted to take every part of her, regardless of the consequences.

What was wrong with him? He'd controlled himself under more pressing circumstances, turned away temptation with little thought.

You have got to temper these feelings!

He could do this—hold to his conviction to keep her safe. All he had to do was remember the possible harm. No joining, and he wouldn't allow her to complete the spell. He grimaced at the thought. Mianna had handled it fine. But in Anna's state, he wondered. What would it do to her if she performed it on a Meridian, anyway? She wouldn't be prepared for the experience. The shock could be traumatic, even harmful.

What was he thinking? It would *not* go that far. He set his mind. *No, it will not come to that.*

She turned back to him and it nearly destroyed his conviction. Her full breasts gleamed with moisture, nipples puckered as the water trickled over them. She looked at him, a question in her gaze.

He cleared his throat and stepped in, fully clothed.

"Um, Anna?" He couldn't keep his gaze from following the water down her body. The heady ignition of lust hit him. Meer inches separated them. His heart thumped. Blood pooled deep in his groin. He cleared his throat again and decided to forgo words. He couldn't make intelligent conversation if he had to.

He reached for the soap and then slid it up her arm with silky ease. It left a glistening trail as he led it over her collar bone. Pinching his lips between his teeth, he guided the suds around the curve of her bosom.

"We don't need to rush this." His whisper came before he realized he'd spoken.

She closed her eyes and leaned her head back as her body relaxed beneath his touch.

Her open acceptance flowed through him. Her awakening emotions welcomed his attention, beckoned him to her. His control waned.

His throat went dry and he held his breath as the sweet lavender soap slipped from his hand. It *clunked* on the marble floor as suds washed from her skin and then slid toward the silver drain together.

One touch. Gently cupping her breast, he lifted it to torture his thirst. *Only a taste...to sedate the craving.* His lips parted.

Restraint fled and he grabbed her waist, pulling her to him. Slick skin pressed against a thread barrier and the fact that the barricade forbade their joining made it that much more enticing.

His conscience offered weak rebuke. *Too much.*

He paid no heed, lost in the pleasure of having her. All the years he'd dreamed of their love, their hunger, condensed into that instant. Intoxicated by the moment, he brushed his lips along her cheek to meet her with an eager kiss. A sweet squeak accompanied a hitch in her breath. Her tongue glided along his in perfect harmony.

Water cascaded through their hair, drumming a mesmerizing rhythm. Easing her against the shower wall, he lowered his body and relished the friction as it brushed along hers.

As she pressed into his movement, a warning flashed across his mind, *Wrong thing to do!*

His tongue swirled the water from the dip of her neck and he savored the nectar with a growl of defiance.

She cried with delectation and tilted her head, dainty breaths pressing her bosoms tighter against his chest.

His voice followed her dainty tone, raspy and led by hunger. "Gods, I want you."

As her knee rose to meet his hip, control drowned. Need raged and he slipped his hand down her hip and around to her inner thigh.

I can stop it before the spell takes effect. I can break the symbol when it's formed. I can...

Anna's leg tightened around him, pressing her hips hard against his groin. Her hands flew to his back, fingers and thumbs forming a triad.

Stop now! The symbol is formed.

Cole struggled to withhold his advance but his hunger, unquenched, turned ravenous. A growl ripped from his chest.

Air rushed into her lungs as she arched her back.

You must stop it now!

"*Unsigh*," cried Anna and inhaled another exclamatory breath.

The spell charged deep into his heart as it began its course to his soul. Tiny spangles of purity delivered reverberations of the ecstasy she rode. It threw him to a time long ago, to their union and consummation.

No, Cole. Don't do this to her, his conscience cried. *As soon as she calls the second part of the spell, your emotions will be added to the experience. If you love her, you'll stop it now!*

In a fit of forced severing, he pushed himself away and broke the triadic symbol. He fell against the back wall of the shower and shuddered as he grasped for the ledge of the tub.

Her cry filled the little room. "*Colhart!*"

Clenching his jaw to repel his intense craving, he hissed through his teeth. "Gods, Anna."

Waves of euphoria echoed from her as she slowly slid to the bottom of the tub.

Cole grunted to vent his arrest. He wiped his hand down his face and then looked at her rapturous countenance. He shook his head. Elaina will have to take his place next time. This couldn't happen again.

Chapter Nineteen

Cole trudged down the hall of the east wing. Trails of water followed every step and his boots squished with tiny bubbles from the saturated soles. Ignoring the tendrils of hair that clung to his cheeks, he followed his uneasy stride toward his room.

James trotted down the stairs to the second landing and then halted with a jolt. "What happened to you?"

Glancing at him, Cole heaved a sigh. "Dear, *Gods,* James. Anna wanted to bathe."

The dimples in James' cheeks deepened, as he seemed to struggle to hold back his chuckle. It burst out anyway. "Don't tell me. You helped her take a shower—in your clothes."

"I'd do more than what I did if I hadn't."

"And," James crossed his arms over his broad chest and failed to conceal his mirth. "Did the clothes help?"

"Barely."

"You know, there's nothing wrong with being with her. But I'd be careful with her performing Mianna's spell. In her condition, use of it on a Meridian could be too much for her."

"My thoughts exactly. But, do you realize how much control it took to stop it when it got to that point? Even with," he held out his soaked sleeves, "this I was lucky to end it when I did."

James lowered his gaze. "I see."

Cole sighed and let his hands fall to his side. "Besides, I know she's only responding to my touch. It's all instinctive. I want it to be more than that." He shook his hands, causing his sleeves to flap around his arms. "I need a drink."

"Well, you're getting the carpet all wet."

He scoffed. "I'm really worried about the carpet right now."

With a grin, James fanned his hands. Cole's saturated wear snapped into crisp threads as the water evaporated and left him dry. He smoothed his hair, combing the strands with his fingers. "Thanks."

"You'd better put off that drink. We have company." James set his hands at his waist. "It seems Elaina's sister is here for a visit."

"What?"

"That's right. I've already sent Elaina to talk with her in the parlor and Vincent is pacing the study. I was running you down to join us. You didn't answer my call."

Cole glanced at his watch. Dry now, but surely soaked from the shower when James tried to contact him. First chance, the scrys would get a protective charm against moisture.

James turned for the stairs. "And Cole, she might already know about our nature."

A glower tugged at his face.

Upon entering the study, Cole silenced the room and quickly took his seat.

Vincent paced the length of the room jaw set and fists clinched. Sparks crackled along his fingers.

James drew his hand over the Utopian and the image of Elaina and Linda appeared. Their attention turned to the hologram forms of the two sisters in conversation on the sofa.

Elaina stroked her older sister's hair and tilted her head in an empathetic gesture. "Linda, he can't do that. Jarrett has never taken an interest in the girls. He won't keep them from you."

"You don't understand, Elaina." Linda lifted from the hug and tears streamed her face.

"I understand that any court will return them to their mother."

She shook her head and sobs accentuated her words. "He's been...cheating for years. All this time, Elaina, he's had someone else! He broke the vow. Our marriage wasn't even a marriage all this time. He said he was leaving to be with her. He took my girls!"

Elaina flushed. "He can't do that."

"He can! By law, he *can*." Linda gasped and covered her mouth, crying into her sleeve-covered hands. "Any court will award children to a couple over a single parent. I've lost my girls."

Elaina threw her arms around her sister and Linda held her tight.

"All I wanted was to turn around and come back for the Shilo's gathering." Her deep sobs jarred her shoulders and Elaina scrunched the back of the cardigan as she tightened her hold. "He just blew up. He didn't want to come to the cookout to begin with, but I bugged him so much he gave in. And when I said I wanted to be with my family when you were welcomed into Vincent's home...he stopped the car and told me about *her*. That *he* was the most important thing to *her*. Not her family. He threw me out. He threw me out, Elaina! On the side of the road!" She pulled back and looked into her little sister's eyes. "He locked the doors and drove away."

Elaina shook her head and stood. Setting her hand at her forehead, she paced the room. "There has to be something we can do. Mandy and Mechenzie belong with you."

Linda wrapped her arms around herself and looked like a weathered puppy. Hiccups punch at her breaths and her shoulders curled forward.

Silence hung in the room and the holograms looked like still life as Elaina stopped at the bar.

Dropping her gaze to her limp fingers, Linda spoke just above a whisper. "Is it true?"

Elaina turned to her. "Huh?"

"Is it really true?" She motioned with her hand. "You know. About the magic in this family?"

Cole threw his head to the side and Vincent's stony countenance flared red.

"Linda," Elaina rushed to her sister and sat at her side. "I never said this family had magic."

"You said Vincent held the magic to your life."

"Well, sure. Love does that."

A little smile crept onto Linda's full lips and she cocked her head. "Let me see. How did you say that? *A magic man has cast a spell on me and I'll be that wizard's wife, whatever it takes.*"

Elaina shook her head so fast her waves bounced around her head. "No, you understood me wrong!"

Blue neon arched before Cole's eyes and flew overhead as Vincent drew his hands to his sides.

Cole jumped to his feet as James lunged for Vincent, but the ribbon of power punched from his fists. Fire flared as the force struck the tapestries like explosives, and shot through the east wall. Shattered lumber flew in the wake as it charged deep into the woodland. Trees plowed to the ground, birds took to flight in flocks, and with the silence enchantment broken on the study, falling planks drummed through the air alongside the rumble of the Shilo Manor foundation.

James whipped his hand skyward and roots rose from the terra to support the failing structure. Vines and limbs snaked across the ceiling and walls, creating a web to hold the framework firm. He threw his thick arms around his enraged brother, pinning his motion.

Vincent's onyx eyes flashed. Power pulsed along his knuckles as he struggled against James' strong hold. Cole scrambled around the desk, summoning chairs, tables, and cabinets to block the entrance should he attempt to face the women in his state. "James! *Do something!*"

With a swoop of his hand, James dispersed into the Smoke of Night, forcing Vincent in his grasp to relinquish form. The dark mass surged like a torrential storm, jets of blue lightning shooting in a madcap frenzy around the room. Books flew, ancient urns shattered, and with devastating impact, the shelves over the hearth failed. Crystal containers crashed to the floor, releasing contained magic of the centuries. Hues of purple and gold shrouded the mantle. Sparks spangled along the wispy crests as they converged.

Before a disaster could arise, Cole threw his fist toward the mass and flicked his fingers into a tight claw. An urgent command punched from his lungs. "*Nuerta!*"

A pale cloud burst from his palm and overtook the ancient ingredients, nullifying the spells. As the hues dispersed, he gazed back at his brother's battling essences. Anger and determination emitted from both souls.

In a rush, a cyclonic barrier surrounded an inner core. The rampant center flared to blinding strobes. Before Cole could shield his eyes, the dark mass bolted out the gaping wreckage into the forest.

Dust and debris fluttered as quiet filled the room. The sudden change rang in Cole's ears and he barely heard the shrill voice. A bolt pierced his heart.

Anna!

Darting for the door, he flung his hand through the air. Blockage tumbled across the floor and out of his way. Ignoring Elaina and Linda's exclamations of an earthquake, he rushed through the foyer and bounded up the steps. Anna sat curled in the corner at the end of the hall, hands over her head. "Anna! You're safe. I'm here."

Her gaze snapped to him. As he ran for her, she scrambled to her feet. He scooped her into his arms and she melted against him, grasping the back of his shirt.

Instant contentment flowed from her emotions and he heaved a breath to settle his nerves. The scent of roses filled him.

A smile lifted the corners of his mouth as he exhaled. She'd spent time savoring the blooms he'd brought her. The fact set sweetly on his soul. He brushed his lips across her cheek, following the aroma. Oh, that it had been because they were from him and not simply that they were flowers.

An arm flew around his shoulder and he peeked over Anna's head to find Elaina embracing them both. Love echoed from her senses as she breathed, "Oh, you guys are okay. Vince and James?"

Cole straightened and cleared his throat. "They're busy taking care of a...mess."

From his periphery, he caught Linda slowly step toward them. He shifted his gaze to watch as she neared. Her tear-streaked face looked doughy, then her jaw dropped open and her blue gaze focused on the woman in his arms. Amidst the emotional trauma and alarming events, one word passed her lips.

"Anna?"

Chapter Twenty

Linda watched every move Cole made as he led Anna back to her room. He sensed Linda's shock at the unrecognized friendship and picked up on feelings of confusion and accusation as she glared at him.

Elaina buzzed around them, pulling back the blankets and straightening Anna's skewed gown. She smiled at the angelic face and helped her lie down, then tucked the downy comforter around her. She sat at her side.

Cole simply stood, holding a calm presence to reassure his love that all was well. He kept his gaze on hers as it flitted back to him each time Elaina passed between them.

"Anna, honey, everything is fine. Vincent and James are taking care of things. Is there anything you need?" Elaina's soft voice seemed to be ignored as Anna's attention was riveted on Cole. With no answer to her question, she looked up at him.

"Why don't you and Linda wait in the parlor?" He stepped to the bedside. "I'll have a talk with her."

Elaina nodded and motioned to her sister as she headed to the hall. Linda sent another accusing glare his way and then followed.

Cole sat beside her and brushed his fingers along her hair. "There was a lot of noise. Upsetting things. But don't worry. It's under control."

She watched him as if to memorize every expression he made. He knew he had to look careworn. But the way she was looking at him, anyone would think he was the most beautiful thing she'd seen.

He smiled. "You liked the roses."

She smiled back and looked at the brilliant buds on the table. "They're beautiful. And soft."

Nodding, he leaned close. "I can smell them on your face. You've been enjoying them."

Turning, she touched her lips to his. "Yes," she whispered.

He gently kissed her, allowing the tender moment to flow through his senses.

She placed her hand to his face and held him there. Her sweet tongue lighted across his lips like a feather and he answered her call, parting them to afford deeper affection. He swept his fingers over her damp hair, pulling her closer.

Her kiss was a lullaby to his soul. Longing pounded into him and desire returned. Centuries of loneliness melted away as he again became lost in her attention. Every caress led him home, back to his place beside her heart. The warm breeze of Zephyrus connected the severed link and Cole basked in the Arylinite nurturing that filled him.

"I love you, Anna." The words passed his lips without censorship and when he heard them, he looked at her unsure of the reaction he'd receive.

Purity of an angel stared back at his wondering gaze. With adoration spilling from her emotions, she pulled him closer and kissed him. Deeply. Lovingly. And he could have sworn he had her whole heart.

He breathed her in, willing it to be so. "Tell me you love me, too, Anna. Tell me I have your heart."

"I love you, too. You have my heart."

The words adorned her whisper, falling onto his lips. Too perfectly recited. Too perfectly an answer to his bid.

He slowly pulled away and took her hands in his. To expect anything else had been foolish. He hoped his disappointment didn't show. Brushing his fingertips across her cheek, he smiled.

Hushed voices drifted from the hall and Cole looked to the half-closed door. He widened his perception to pick up as much of the conversation that he could. Linda's voice hissed with low tones.

"What is Anna doing here? She was all over the Morning Post clinging to Lord Dressen's arm like they were the couple of the year. He was even on the news bragging about the elaborate stained-glass privacy screens she presented to him at his birthday celebration."

Elaina's response topped a whisper, but Cole deciphered her soprano utterance easily. "Stained-glass? Wait, isn't that what Dad had to finish up when—oh, this is *that* Anna? The one we thought disappeared?"

"Evidently she disappeared right into His Lordship's arms. I knew all those rumors about the curfew were rubbish."

"Linda, the guys found her last night. She'd been hurt badly. Her dress was torn and bloody and she was really out of it. Cole saved her. He's helping her cope. If it wasn't for him, she'd be dead."

"If she was on her death bed, how is she able to run through the house today? She looks pretty healthy to me."

"I saw her Linda. I helped tend to her... Why would Lord Dressen do that?"

"He wouldn't. He's been after her for years." She huffed, but sadness flowed. "I can't believe she didn't tell me. We've been best friends for so long."

"Aw, Linda, I'm sorry. She's just really confused right now."

Linda's voice softened. "Well, it looks like he finally got to her."

Cole looked at his love. Serenity poured from her as she sat with her hands in her lap and quietly watched him. The corners of her cute lips slowly curved up at his attention and couldn't he help but return the action. He added a little wink and a full smile blossomed for him. A chuckle puffed from his nostrils.

"Something had to have happened after the party," Linda continued. "And you didn't answer my question. How did she get well so fast?"

Elaina didn't answer and Cole imagined a lowered gaze as the young lady tried to think of what to say.

Linda's voice picked up volume as she pressed the subject. "It is true. They are magical. As stupid as it sounds, wizards actually exist. Just like you said, a wizard's wife. That's the only explanation if what you're telling me is true... So, is it true? Are they wizards?"

"I'm not saying that."

"You don't have to. Your face says it all. They could help me get Mandy and Mechenzie back."

Cole sensed panic as Elaina shot her response. "My face isn't saying anything. Just leave it alone. I was just running my mouth about how I felt about Vince. Nothing more."

"Elaina, talk to them. They know you. Tell them to help me."

"No!" She gasped. "I mean they can't break the law, can they? Others would know."

Okay, this has gone far enough. Cole leaned to Anna and spoke softly. "I need to go take care of some things. Get some rest, and I'll be back later."

Her eyes widened and she sat up straight. "You'll be back later? After I get some rest?"

"How could I stay away?" Stroking her dark brown hair, he tore himself from the pull of her spirit and stepped into the hall.

The sisters stood at the top of the stairs, Elaina against the banister, gripping it with her fists.

Linda narrowed her eyes. "What are you afraid of?" She slowly nodded. "It's a secret, isn't it? That they're wizards. That's why you're here. They made you come stay until the wedding."

"It's customary to stay with the Nobles before the Chalice ceremony."

"Well, someone has to tell Lord Dressen Anna's okay. He must be worried sick."

Creases etched across Elaina's brow. "I don't know, Linda. I think we should leave it to the guys."

"Why? So they can get the favor? If I bring him the news, *he* might help me get my girls back. Forget the guys if they won't help family. I'll go right to a lawmaker."

A block formed in Cole's chest and he lifted his chin, ready to do what it took to ensure silence on the matter.

"They don't need his favors! I just think they should handle this." Elaina scampered down the stairs and Linda hurried after her.

"And I need to handle getting my babies back. I won't let Jarrett take them from me. Can't you understand that? I won't! I'll do anything to get them back. Anything!"

Cole marched to the landing. His voice boomed through the foyer. "Nobody's telling Dressen."

The two spun to meet his stern gaze. His jaw clenched and he bore his ebony glare on them.

Elaina's shoulders scrunched and tears sheened her eyes. "No, Cole. Of course we wouldn't say anything." She sent her gaze to her sister's glower. "Linda just doesn't understand."

"I understand I have more to gain here than anyone by bringing him the news." She looked at Cole, her brows pressed together. "You've nursed her, now let her go home. I know he must be looking for her."

"We're taking care of the situation. And we'll handle it as we see fit."

Linda shook her head, disbelief crossing her determined features.

"You'll both go to the parlor and wait for Vincent to come get you."

Elaina grabbed Linda's hand and trotted down the marbled-capped stairs. Linda tripped after as she was tugged. Quick taps sounded through the receiving hall as they bustled across the floor. The door slammed behind them.

A growl rumbled in Cole's throat. He needed Vincent to handle his future sister-in-law. Glancing down the hall toward the study, his scowl deepened. And he needed James to fix the runt's mess.

Cole closed the door to the study and stepped into the foyer. All was quiet. His slow stride clunked against the hardwood floor and shuffled to a stop beside his brother.

He looked hard at James as he leaned against the banister. Irritation gathered across his face in stark contrast to his usual mild demeanor. It took considerable doing to ruffle this brother into disgruntlement.

He glanced around the room to find words of comfort. "You did a fine job restoring the damage. The chandelier doesn't even look tarnished."

This didn't seem to ease the tension flowing from him.

James looked at him from the corner of his eyes. "That mantle held irreplaceable items. Most came from Meridian."

Cole glanced back to the study. "Forget about the mantle. We haven't used most of that magic for years."

No response.

Cole pursed his lips and scratched his chin. *Change the topic.* He motioned to the parlor. "They think it was a mild quake. Kid still in the woodland?"

"Vincent will be staying there until he calms down enough to deal with the situation."

"Can *you* deal with this?"

"I'll deal with this. Different subject matter."

"Well, the woman's a threat to our plan with Anna." Cole repositioned himself and folded his arms. "She wants to turn her over to Dressen in exchange for custody of her girls." He took a heavy breath. "And she's convinced we're wizards. I heard them on the stairs. She was badgering Elaina. That girl never meant to tell Linda anything. The emotions I picked up were exactly the way she sounded in the parlor earlier. Shock. Elaina can't believe what she said about Vince was taken literally." He shook his head. "Linda drew her own conclusions."

James set his hands at his waist. "This isn't good." He looked at him and leaned his head into a leer, dimpling his cheek as his lips tightened. "And don't even think about tampering with her memory. Partial removal causes more harm than good."

Cole raised his brows. "Actually, I wasn't considering partial memory removal."

"No." James pointed a finger, accentuating his charge. "You're not wiping her memory. We will *not* cross that line."

"Then what do you propose? We're at a loss here, James."

He shifted his stand, looking to the side. "I don't know. We need to insist she stay as our guest. Buy some time so we can figure this all out."

Cole raked a hand over his hair. "She'll try to talk to Anna. She recognized her. I believe they were friends."

"I'll keep an eye on her."

"Look, James. I know you mean well but with what she knows she's a true threat. It's justifiable."

"No!"

Cole threw his head to the side.

"I'll watch her." James' eyes flashed with his words. "You just concentrate on Anna. Get things in order so we can unbind her soul as soon as possible."

He nodded, taking an apprehensive breath. "I'm about there. But Kid will need to calm down before all this happens. I'll have enough emotion to deal with coming from her without adding his temper to it."

"I'll prepare something to help you cope." James dropped his arms to his side and headed for the parlor. "You just worry about getting the spells right."

Chapter Twenty-One

A cool breeze washed across Cole's face as he sat beneath the apricot tree in the front yard. Dim lights of the city cast a weak halo on the skyline, a sad contrast to the once-vivid spectacle of nightlife. Their metropolis looked old, withered. Bitterness gnawed at him. *The curfew.* Was the law just a step in Dressen's plot to get what he wanted? How else could he ensure that they would consider an individual with a home and a job their next potential harvest subject?

He drank a lengthy swig of liqueur from the bottle in his hand. The strong mix seared his throat and heat pulsed through his chest. He growled the sensation away. Leaning against the tree trunk, he crossed his ankles and scowled. The ancient covenant gave the lawmakers the right to run their domain as they saw fit. But to abuse the power for personal gain breached the gods' intent—how could he have allowed time to influence his view of the matter?

The noblemen's gradual pursuit of power over others echoed the actions of their fathers. And Sylis

Shilo had ultimately paid the price for their greed. Cole slugged another take from his drink and sent a disgruntled gaze to the city.

Mankind seemed doomed to repeat the same deeds. Short lives allowed unawareness. Warnings in history books turned into tales told at the bedsides of babes. They wouldn't learn from their fathers' mistakes.

Light from the front door pierced the darkness and James stepped onto the porch. Cole set his drink down at his side and coughed to catch his attention.

"There you are." He walked to the end of the porch and down the steps. "What are you doing out here? I figured you'd be in the lab."

"I needed some fresh air." He glanced at his watch. Ten-thirty p.m. "It's nice out tonight."

His brother eased to the ground and set his arms on his knees. "I talked Linda into staying for a while, told her to pick out some new clothes from Bryman's catalogue since Jarrett left her with nothing. A seamstress will come and tailor-fit them for her. She seemed happy with the idea. I assigned her a room near mine so I could keep tabs."

Cole nodded. "She's not going to set this aside."

James looked out over the view.

"You know what it'll come down to, James."

"She's not a subject, Cole. She has a home at her parents' and she has children."

Cole sighed and took another drink. He grunted. "What about a partial spell? A mild bending of will. It wouldn't have to be a full take. Just enough to get her to look at our side of the situation."

James leaned back onto his hands. "How would that make us any different from the Grand Marshals knowing what we know now? They abused their powers to get what they wanted. If we start bending wills to make people agree with us, we're no better than they are."

"We've already done that. How many people have we subjected to their will since we learned what's going on?"

"They were needy and willing. The lords provide security for dedicated service."

"Anna wasn't needy!" He spat the words, unable to withhold his venom. Pangs of regret curdled his stomach as her frightened image shown bright in his memory. "Or willing," he added with a deep frown. "This whole curfew law was set to lead up to her capture."

James frowned. "I thought of that. And you're right. Dressen led the way in getting the bill passed. But we can't resort to their way of thinking. We've done enough of that. We've worked a Cornerstone post longer than any other sentinel. We can't let character traits influence us further."

Resentment boiled in Cole's stomach. "We've worked this post longer than any other." He scoffed. "As if we had a choice." His father's fate passed through his mind, grazing the painful vision of the locked portal.

He looked at his brother. He could hardly make out his profile as he sat five feet from him. It was so dark under this realm's night cover. Nostalgia tugged at his heart. Meridian's five moons ensured a constant glow of light indigo as they reflected blue sun rays over their home. Even at night, it was bright enough to see without aid.

James leaned forward, setting his arms on his knees again. "When they deem it time, there'll be another portal." His voice was low and Cole knew he intended it as comfort, but he couldn't help feel forgotten by the gods. He looked away sickened by the thought.

A rattle came from the door and they turned their attention to the porch. Linda quickly hopped outside and scampered down the steps. She rushed across the wide lawn to the iron gates at the end of the drive, slipped through them, and then headed toward town.

Cole smiled. And downed the rest of his drink. "Well, what do you know, the next harvest subject." He stood and strode to the front door. "Get Kid and meet me on the porch in thirty minutes. I need to brief you on what's about to happen."

He glanced out at the dull city lights. No doubt, she'd use the park as a shortcut. He stretched out his hand, holding it there a moment then snapped his fingers into a fist, closing Gryffin's city gateway. It would serve them well again.

The potpourri of spring blossoms met Cole as he billowed his essence to reform in the shadows of Shilo Park. His brothers took their place at his side and he gazed through the dark city green.

Linda gazed up at the granite god sitting on the meridian cap. "Gryffin?" Her voice was filled with innocence. She grasped the iron bars forming the gates. "God of Conformance, I need your help."

Cole waited in light of the entreaty.

"I've always given you reverence. I've prayed to you even in the best of times. I never asked for..." She paused and stared up at the gargoyle that sat motionless on the heavy arch.

Cole followed her gaze to the large likeness. The great creature was at least five feet tall, lounging on his forelegs. His feline backside hunched into a crouch, his broad rump rounding from the meticulously carved feathers that cloaked his back. Wings tucked to his side and laid flat against his torso, arching from his shoulders in a steep heart. His tail curled around his hindquarters and rested beside long talons that gripped the edge of the structure on the other side. Thick brows dipped severely into his round eyes, revealing the predatory personality of such a beast. The tip of his hooked beak rested just above his fledged chest as if angling down to watch as she pleaded.

Cole knew the appearance well. Though intimidating in rock form, it didn't come close to the awe-striking appearance when he took life.

Linda caught her breath and rushed to the side of the walkway. Gathering a handful of lilies, she returned and held them up as in offering. "Gryffin," she cried. "Protector! I beg you find favor with your child."

Silence filled the air as her beseeching gaze traced the idol of her world. Cole felt the hush emanate from his brothers as they watched a child of Terra plead with her god.

James leaned to Cole's ear. "Don't give her time to lose faith Cole. You know as well as I do Gryffin won't open those gates for her. She's a strong-willed woman who is willing to fight for the ones she loves. She doesn't deserve this moment."

Linda lowered her hands. Turning, she slid along the bars to the ground.

"Linda, stand tall."

Surprise and hope covered her face. She scrambled to a stand and gazed up at the great stone griffin.

He stepped into his stride; James and Vincent flanked him. Their steps echoed through the empty park. She whipped around and peered into the heavy shadows that filled the path. Her face drew shock and she backed away, only to be blocked by the locked gates of the north entrance.

"Gryffin?" Her whispered prayer fell weak. She wavered and slid to the ground again.

As they neared, Cole stepped forward while Vincent and James held their stand a step behind.

Linda's eyes grew wide. "Cole?" Her voice trembled. "W-what's going on?"

"You're out after curfew."

"Y-you enforce the curfew?" Her hands trembled with her voice. "I...I thought...it was just..." She released a quick breath.

"There are things you don't understand." He looked into her blue eyes and slowly lifted his hand. A pale pink mist filled the air. "But you will."

Her mouth fell slack and she blinked away tears as the enchantment flowed past her lips. She stood, resignation replacing fear. Contentment flowed from every fiber of her being.

Cole slid his arm around her waist and glanced at his watch. *"Lord Dressen is expecting you."*

Lifting his hand, he dispersed them into the Smoke of Night. Her senses flew alongside his, mollified, subjective.

He headed north to the prestigious neighborhood of Grand Marshals.

Chapter Twenty-Two

The stained-glass windows around Lord Dressen's arched doors glowed bright. Without hesitation, Cole guided them through the keyhole of the grand door, a condensed black mass snaking into the foyer.

Dressen appraised their arrival like a king from his throne, seated in a high-back chair at the center of the room. He tapped his forefinger on the armrest.

Cole grasped their accumulated essences and forced them to form a giant billow, rising beyond the second floor level. Confusion flashed from his brothers' emotions as they lost control of their elements. As expected, James swelled in protest and Vincent emitted a spangle of quick strobes through their bulging cloud. Cole snapped their forms together just beyond the threshold. The instant scowls hidden by their disembodiment took form, relaying the message he wanted to aim at the pompous fiend.

They were not happy.

A heavy scent of licorice accompanied a flash of ebony in the lord's eyes and Cole couldn't hold back a second glance. Images from his dream littered his mind. He pushed the thoughts aside, tightened his hold on Linda's waist. She leaned into him beneath his cloak.

"You requested a harvesting to be delivered by midnight."

Lord Dressen stood. "I did."

Cole looked him in the eyes as he listed the original requirements of the bid. "A curfew breaker from the city's east side. Approximate age, twenty-five. Approximate height, five feet five inches. Complexion, light. Will bent to total compliance. Position to be filled, upstairs—*maid*." He emphasized the final word and pulled aside his cape to reveal Linda standing wide-eyed before him.

A growl rumbled in Dressen's chest as he clenched his fists. "What is this?"

"A refilling of your harvest order."

"That isn't Anna!"

Cole tilted his head. "The order didn't specify the subject's name to be Anna."

Dressen's face flushed red. "I wanted Anna then and I want her now!"

"Are you telling me you had a certain person in mind when you placed this order?"

Tension poured from his brothers. James' anger pulsed beneath a tight band of composure and Vincent's rage boiled. Heat coursed under Cole's skin as he held fast to indignation.

Silence hung in the air.

James' hand eased into Cole's periphery and took Linda by the arm. Her stunned gaze didn't veer from Dressen as she followed his lead to stand behind him.

Dressen cocked his brow and he closed the gap between them with meandering steps.

"Are you telling me that an ancient, all-powerful wizard such as Cole Shilo hadn't come to that conclusion upon receipt of such an order?" He cocked a grinned. "I was sure you instilled her with that little extra prize precisely for that reason."

Cole furrowed his brow. *The binding?* Surely, he didn't speak of that. He filtered through his mind to connect any oddity other than innocence, lack of depth, or indecision—all traits that could fall under the bid of total compliance.

Dressen pursed his lips. "I was delighted with the results. But do tell me. What does Unsigh mean? The experience is phenomenal." He waved a dismissing hand. "Short lived after she says Colhart, but..." He chuckled then a sudden accusatory flare crossed his face. He stepped directly in front of Cole.

"Colhart." He folded his arms across his chest. "Tell me Sir Cole. You're not native to Terra. What is your given name?" There was no quizzical tone in his question. Total knowledge filled every word as he pronounced each syllable.

Cole squared his shoulders. "Colhart Nixtoro Krylu Shilomacj."

A grin lit Dressen's lips. "Colhart. Nixtoro. Krylu. Shilomacj." He turned and paced a small distance then looked back at the three and nodded. "It seems the Wizards of Shilo Manor have taken on their own rules for the services they perform to the Lords of Terra."

Vincent flared red. "We've done no such thing!" Sparks danced around his tight fists and he marched a step beside Cole. James followed suit, creating an undeniable stand of support beside him.

"Adding to an order to dispel complete satisfaction?" Dressen stepped back to them and grabbed Cole's wrist. Clasping his hand, he forced his palm to envelope the pearl. "You wanted her? How about a vision of what you're missing."

He grabbed Cole's wrist and forced his palm to envelope the pearl. Images overtook his inner eye; Anna's hooded gaze, dark hair askew on the pillow. The scent of rose soap swam in the air. He buried his face in the soft locks at her neck and grazed her skin with his teeth. His touch glided down the curve of her hip as her thigh pressed hard against his side. Heat swirled through his biceps, charged down his torso and rammed at his groin.

Legs weakening, he wavered as the enhanced experience overtook him. James grasped his shoulders, bracing his stand.

Edged rapture burned in Cole's core as the vision continued. Anna's hands flew to his back. Her fingers and thumbs pressed together, forming the triad. With a cry in her breath, she uttered the words intended only for him. The command echoed in his ears, resonated in his heart. Her passion flew through him. Fire blazed and waves of ecstasy forced instinct to take his body. Gasping, he doubled over.

A growl punched from Cole's lungs and he whipped his hand from Dressen's grip. "*Enough!*"

The lord's anger boomed through the room. "You want her! You wanted her and in your haste to get her back you made one fatal mistake."

Cole clenched his teeth to gain control of his state. He glanced at the lawman's glare and then shifted his gaze to the lavender pearl pressed tightly between his fingers. Spells, potions, the attention he poured into the creation of the gift filed through his mind. He'd followed each precise detail of his father's records. Where could he have failed?

"I suspected your involvement from the onset. I suspected, but couldn't prove. Not until I realized I held the answer in my pocket."

Dressen snatched the pearl into his fist. "Every memory relived in stark detail. You expected me to revel in the simple enhanced memories of my life." He jabbed his fist toward Cole and the magical gift glowed, illuminating his fingers. "*You underestimated me, Colhart Nixtoro Krylu Shilomacj!* What made you think I wouldn't recall every experience touching my senses as I relived the moment I first explored the gift?"

He threw his hand in the direction of the terrace. "I felt the change in atmosphere as you sent her the spell, smelled the ginger in the very potion you used. I heard Anna gasp, run, and I heard you turn straightway and leave when the deed was done."

Cole's mind whirled. No Terran should have detected such detail beyond the intended recollection of moments. Nor should they have the ability to share the intricate detail of the memory called upon. Worse yet, none should have experienced the intimate nature of the spell he'd created for Mianna. The memory Dressen shared was indeed the full extent of the gift. He struggled to harness the effects it had on him.

Dressen shoved the pearl into his pocket. "You stole my subject after payment was received." With a swift turn, he grabbed an onyx pillar and heaved it cross the room. It rammed into the velveteen chair and both skidded to the far side of the room.

"You crossed the wrong Grand Marshal! The counsel has viewed the evidence. I showed them every bit of the memory. All agree to your guilt and proceedings are underway. *You will pay, Cole Shilo!*"

Vincent snarled and lightening charged from his fingertips.

"*No, Kid! He's protected by the covenant.*" Cole dove for him as a second burst flew.

The magical charges rebounded off the lord as if invisible armor sealed his body. Scattering in madcap disarray around the room, they struck the marble staircase. Balusters wheeled through the air with chunks of white and black rock. A fracture traveled up the length of the flight. Iron groaned as the inner pitch strained. Marble hammered to the floor and as the second floor landing shifted, the grand stained-glass window jarred.

Time seemed to slow as the myriad of shapes and colors cascaded to the floor. Glass shattered in a continuous roar and Cole squeezed his lids shut in an attempt to lessen the impact on his ears. Frigid air whisked debris around the upper scope of the room. Screams filtered through the din and he peeked to the second level hallways. Servants peered around the walls and then darted back the way they came.

Rage burned in Dressen's eyes as his deep voice carried on the torrent. "You *dare* attack a Grand Marshal? Those you are here to serve?"

James' jaw flexed as he clenched it tight. His upper lip curled and with a single step, he widened his stance. Cole held to Vincent to brace himself. He could count on one hand the times he'd seen that look on his eldest brother, and each time had resulted in cyclonic disaster.

Drawing his thick arms in an all-encompassing circle, James' biceps bulged. The wind obeyed his command. Chairs, tables, onyx pillars, and portraits swept from their stays and swirled into a twister.

Dressen's hair slapped at his brow. His clothes clapped against his body. Leaning into the current, he grasped the left balustrade and clung tight. The netted crystals from the wall whirled to life. Swooping around the lawmaker, they lifted him to the wall. The tiny gems dug deep into the side panels, pinning him eight feet above the floor.

James marched over to the trapped sire. "We serve none other than the gods of the realms! Our purpose here is to aid in keeping peace within the spectrum. If force is the only way to accomplish that, then so be it. We will *not* be used to satisfy the pleasures of noblemen. Set forth your trials. We will not be moved until Gryffin, Taravaughn, and Arylin deem it so. The covenants stand!"

He lowered his voice to a stern warning. "Call your assemblies and bid all to pray for mercy. By condoning your actions, it is the Grand Marshalls who have broken the covenant as you have."

Dressen's fingers flexed through the holes in the net. A low growl rode his sneer.

Releasing Vincent, Cole stood tall. "We're finished here."

Quick strides brought James to Linda and he wrapped his arm around her shoulders, pulling her close. With a furl of their cloaks, they dispersed into the Smoke of Night. Intensifying their billowed essence to a thick ball of energy, Cole crashed through the doors. The mansion's stained-glass face pulverized and as objects crashed to the receiving hall floor, pounding echoed through the estate grounds.

Shilo City's tall buildings passed in a blur as Cole's speed fed off their joined anger. His fatigued mind whirled with adrenalin, determination, and purpose.

Zipping over the east side commerce district, Shilo Park came to view. Movement caught his senses and he spared it meager attention. An electric charge shot through his essence as he realized the cause and his brother's elements stumbled into a sloppy halt around him.

Massive wings arched skyward and beat at the darkness. Treetops bent from the disturbance. A great eagle's head stretched high, the hooked beak opened, and an ancient cry pierced the air. Birds took to flight, flocks of flutters blocking their view.

Another shrieking roar echoed and Cole shifted to keep his line of sight. Large talons bit chunks of rock from the north entrance. Gravel rained to the footpath. Hind claws dug into the stone arch and the griffin vaulted to the pavement. The asphalt gave way beneath his weight.

He gazed around the empty city and shook off the sediment of time. With a swish of his long tail, he turned. Dislodged rock crunched beneath his feet as he walked through the open gates. Leaping into the air, the eight-foot wings spread wide.

Cole watched the night sky swallow the gargoyle. His senses stung. Hadn't he just considered the number of times Gryffin had taken the form of his likeness? Eternal consequences had hung in the balance.

Forcing his thoughts to his brothers, he darted for Shilo Manor. *"The unbinding must take place tonight."*

Chapter Twenty-Three

As soon as they entered Shilo Manor, James veered toward the parlor with Linda. Vincent shot up the stairs, while Cole headed for the study.

Forming outside the threshold, he threw the door wide and marched to stand before the three crystal globes. He sucked in a long stream of air to steady his nerves. Placing his hands on the first, he spoke the spell he had hoped he would never need.

"Triad of Power, parclainum."

The ball glowed bright, beams shooting through the space between his fingers. He repeated the process on the next. As he rested his hands on the third, his palms tingled. Cole caressed the smooth surface, allowing the warmth from within it to fill him. Closing his eyes, he cast the spell on his crystal to call on the gods' power to join theirs.

The light of his globe poured from the bookshelf with the others. Rays gleamed from the shiny surfaces around the room as they reflected the intense illuminations. Magical items around the hearth sparkled and Cole lifted his hand toward the copper memory box. It shot into his palm.

Turning on his heal, he marched out the door. Globes lifted from their plinths and followed. His feet beat the hardwood floor as he sent a pressing message to Vincent's mind. *"You've spoken with Elaina about this?"*

"She knows," he called from the third floor landing.

Holding the bejeweled box in his palm, Cole tilted the lid. Ginger essence trailed behind him as he bound up the stairs. He glanced over the balustrade toward the parlor door. *"James. Now!"*

The command punched from his lungs and thoughts with such urgency, his determination doubled at the sound of it. He snatched at the ginger cloud with a full fist and forced it forward, fingers outstretched. Three balls of light dashed past him, illuminating the hall and washing out the portraits that lined the wall. Cole launched into a run.

Steps hammered overhead, a door slammed below, as the others rushed his way.

Anna's door swung open and the magical items dipped inside. Her gaze snapped to his as he entered. Disheveled hair covered half her face and the gown tugged her shoulder straps at an odd angle. Though crystal balls floated beside her and a ginger aura filled the air, she seemed to notice only him.

Her voice cracked. "You. You chased me down the alley."

He slowly sat on the edge of her bed. "Yes."

Reverence mixed with confusion, and if he wasn't letting his heart get in the way, love flowed from her emotions. "I was terrified. But you brought me peace."

"Anna..."

Shoving the comforter from her legs, she kicked it aside and threw her arms around his shoulders.

"You kissed me and gave me new life."

A heavy sigh issued from Cole's lungs. "You remember very little. That never should have happened…" Unable to withhold his heart, he allowed his breath to finish his statement. "My love."

Vincent and Elaina darted into the room and Anna flinched at the intrusion. As James crossed the threshold, Linda pushed pass him and dove for her.

"Oh, Anna, I'm so sorry. I had no idea."

"What are you talking about?"

James set his large hand on Linda's shoulder. "She doesn't remember everything yet. Your support will mean a great deal. But I ask that you allow us to perform what's necessary to undo all the harm."

He turned to Cole and handed him a small vial. "Put that on your tongue. It will help you cope without the added emotions of others."

The gesture couldn't have come soon enough. He quickly swallowed the contents, ensuring he got every drop. As if bathed in paraffin, a thin layer of hot wax coated his mouth, reaching deep into his throat and lungs. Anxiety disappeared.

He inhaled deeply, looking back at his love. "Anna, I gave you these small memories to awaken your mind to what's missing in your life. Greater moments before the kiss are hidden. Some of them are full of joy and some are filled with sorrow." He took her hands in his. " Right now, you see me as a savior of peace. Your will views me as your Keeper, your guide. That's not life. You must be able to make your own choices."

Anna blinked, question vivid in her gaze. Cole stood and wrapped his hands around his brilliant sphere. Willing it to lessen in intensity, the light softened to a glow. "We are going to return these rights to you. But this isn't going to be easy. You will see things from your past, relive experiences that will be unpleasant."

Vincent motioned with his nod and Elaina rushed around the bed. "But, we'll be here to help however we can, okay?" Linda seemed determined to keep hold of her friend, so Elaina placed her hand on Anna's arm, sitting at her side. "We'll be *right here*. Whatever happens, you can count on us, okay?"

Anna glanced at her. "I don't understand."

James grasped his crystal. "Humanity wasn't meant to be controlled by another. You should grow, learn, experience."

Linda placed her hand on Anna's cheek, guiding her to face her. "Anna, you want to remember your parents, don't you? And you used to be one of the most sought after artisans in the city. My father owes you much more than he pays you."

Elaina laughed, but it came out like a nervous squeak.

Anna slowly nodded as she gazed into her friend's eyes.

Cole watched the compassionate conversation, glad he couldn't pick up on Anna's feelings. The potion, however, couldn't silence the soft words she spoke as she looked back at him. "But...will I still love you?"

The words hung in the air as silence filled the room. The brothers looked away.

"Anna," Cole's voice cracked. He'd assumed every reaction from her had been instinctive, an answer to his bid. Perhaps to this point it was. With the summon of short-term memories could her heart truly have surmised that emotion for him?

Setting aside his feelings, he motioned for Vincent to take hold of his globe. The youngest sentinel reached for the bright ball and Cole sent him mental instruction on how to make it dim. It followed Vincent's command.

Lifting his hand toward Anna, Cole spoke the words to allow her recollection. He lighted memories to her mind and heart as gently as he could. *"Visola compe. Amoria conecho threshjanan."*

He paused as particles burst from his palm and rained on her like silver confetti.

Anna's eyes brightened. "I'm an artist. A stained-glass artist. I used to plaster colored paper on my wall and pretend they were grand windows of a cathedral." A puff of laughter passed her lips. "Mr. Cantrell thought it was a lousy example of my work but he liked the style."

Linda beamed. "Yes! And there are a lot more things to remember." She looked at Cole, blonde brows raised and tear stained cheeks pressed tight with her smile.

James looked at him with a stern gaze and Cole grimaced. He knew he'd have to reveal deeper experiences. He just couldn't bear to begin the whole revelation with loss. Heaving a sigh, he shifted his gaze back to Linda.

"Linda, I want you to hold Anna tightly." He softened his tone. "Please."

Linda's smile faded and she cuddled closer, wrapping her arms around Anna's shoulders.

Elaina held to her arm and grasped the headboard with her other hand. Her forehead tightened, pressing a deep crease over the bridge of her nose. The apprehension in her eyes was clear and Cole couldn't blame her one bit. He'd done this only a few times before, by request of the Lords whose clients didn't comply to their taste. Then, there had been no emotional attachment. Strictly duty. How could he have been so devoid of compassion for them? For that matter, how could he have put them in that situation to begin with?

Closing his eyes, Cole recited the incantation as memorized so long ago.

Screams pierced the air and his lids flew open. He held his hand steady as a dark mist issued from his palm and then swirled, forming into loose images. Distorted faces bulged, ebbed into brick patterns, morphed into tattered clothes. Linda inched away as they encased Anna's legs and spread to entrap her body. Anna clung tighter, kicking at the phantoms. The comforter tumbled from the bed, but the demons remained, soaking into her skin.

Elaina gasped and jumped to her feet, backing against the wall.

As the apparitions soaked into Anna's skin, she shoved Linda away and thrashed across the bed. She grasped at her stomach and rolled to her side. Her face turned crimson as she spewed black purge. Traces of diamond-like glitter sparkled in the sick. Immediately, disgorge took on life and encircled her again.

Elaina threw both hands to her mouth and then buried her face in Vincent's back.

Linda's shrill voice drowned Anna's painful cries. "What's *happening*?"

James' soft tone answered her. "She's refusing her past. Until she accepts it, the process will continue."

A heavy ache throbbed in Cole's heart as he held his ground. He gulped at the thickness in his throat but it refused to shrink. Time seemed senseless. Uncontrollable, uncaring. He scoffed a breath of impatience. He should be holding her, comforting her. Instead he was locked in his stand of authority, causing his love to relive every loss, pain, moment of fear. He inwardly thanked James for his offering of emotional silence. This was unbearable to watch.

Anna released another sparkling heave of bile. Demons from her past attacked her once again.

A soft prayer punctuated the din as Linda cried to her god. "Have mercy. Taravaughn, God of Life, have mercy on your child."

Anna rolled onto her back and threw her hands to her face, bitter sobs punching from her lungs. "I...don't...understand."

Recognizing the final steps of acceptance, Cole freed a heavy breath. "Anna." Their gazes met and his heart sank. Oh, that he could go to her. He cleared his throat to gain control of his senses. "This was your life. Every joy and disappointment. It's what has made you who you are."

"My Keeper, please help me. Tell me what to do."

He shook his head. "That's not how it should be, Anna."

With trembling hands, she reached for him as if beseeching his returned adoration. "But I love you. I *want* you."

A chill traveled up Cole's spine. "What?"

She leaned her head to her shoulder, causing her tears to trail into her messed hair. "I want you. Don't you want me, too?"

She wants? How could that be? At this point, a bound soul should have no such depth. He looked at James who mirrored his surprise.

"Anna." His voice rasped as his mouth dried. Licking his lips, he dropped his gaze to the foot of the bed to regain composure. "At this point, your will is bent. When you were selected to serve under a lord's care, you inhaled a spell that would ensure compliance to his wishes." He glanced at her as she lowered her arms. "Removing this spell will enable you to think clearly. I may not be your...choice."

Pain shadowed her blue eyes and a small sob caused her nostrils to flare.

Averting his gaze, he solemnly spoke the incantation that would remove her from his keep. A fine mist erupted from his palm. White powder lighted on her and then disappeared as her skin drank it in.

Cole watched from his periphery, expecting her to jump from the bed, attempt to escape when she realized she'd been held against her will.

Anna's gaze stayed riveted on him. He flushed. "Anna?"

"You're not my keeper."

"No."

"I don't need a keeper."

"No."

"I have my own will and my wants aren't influenced by anyone."

"Yes."

"Then why do I still want you? Our kiss was the one right thing in my life. And you want to pretend it never happened."

Cole's brow furrowed. It couldn't be possible. All rules of ancient magic pointed to the fact that a kiss following the administration of a spell sealed it. In cases that affected the will, it also merged the soul with the body, binding them together in death. As a result, basic instincts take over to protect when the soul fails to provide guidance. When the keeper isn't present, fears overwhelm, just as she'd reacted the nights she was alone at Dressen's.

Anna shook her head, looking every bit that she'd lost love.

Lowering his hand, he peered back into her teary eyes. There it was again. The call, a beckoning, and he wanted more than ever to set aside every thought and go to her.

"Cole."

James' voice called him from his trance and he pulled his gaze away to look at him. Repeatedly, James had been the voice of logic, offering better advice than his own heart-following head. Damn potion. What were his brother's feelings on the matter? If she could ascertain the thoughts and feelings of want and voice her own concerns…

"The process must be completed."

Cole threw his confusion to James' mind. *"What if her soul wasn't bound, James? She's not acting like it was bound. I removed the bending of will. I'm not her anchor anymore. She should be filled with fear right now."*

Stepping to his side, James placed his hand on Cole's chest. As Cole stepped back, James eased into his place and set his hands at his waist. His cloak blocked Cole from Anna's view.

A gasp sounded and the headboard banged against the wall. "You," cried Anna. "You chased me down the alley! How could you… What did you *do* to me?"

Linda's voice followed quickly. "It's okay, Anna. It's only James. You know, James."

Cole's senses hardened at the reality that played out. *The love that joined us through the ages anchored her, not the spell.*

James sent his gaze over his shoulder. "For her salvation Cole, for what you truly want, this process must be completed."

Clenching his jaw, Cole set his determination and stepped to the side of her bed. Anna released a quick breath and dove for his arms. Sweet relief filled him as he wrapped her in his embrace. Hot puffs of air warmed his shoulder where her cheek rested. Her tangled hair brushed his lips, the scent of roses and sweat lingering on the strands. If only that moment could last.

Gently gripping her upper arms, he pulled away. "Anna, your soul is in danger. Please allow us to complete the procedure that will free it from its binds." He brushed disheveled locks from her face. "I'll be here through it all. I'll be here when it's over."

With a slow nod, Anna shrank onto the mattress. He raised his crystal and James and Vincent join him with theirs. The white globes pulsed and arches burse forth, connecting the three with thin bands, creating a Triad of Power. Conviction burned within him as innocence peered at him from the bed.

"*Optimi opres, Anna Sinclair, ganton revite.*"

Rays streamed through the gaps between their fingers and brightness washed out Cole's vision. He squinted his eyes to control the intensity. Sparks of red ash littered the air. "*Queltahj emorous. Queltahj emorous.*"

Arcs of deep crimson formed within the haze and then jutted from the globes. Anna screamed. The bed shook with the rustle of sheets.

Linda's plea rode the commotion. "Have mercy. Taravaughn, God of Life, have mercy."

Glass shattered. Gusts thrashed at the curtains and they whipped from the windows, whirling through the room. Paintings banged against the walls and then rammed into the dresser and armoire. The corner chair tumbled across the floor.

A tall funnel formed to Cole's left and he blinked, trying to decipher the activity. Before he could acknowledge Taravaughn's presence, Anna released a wail from deep within her chest.

A voice of thunder shook his soul. *"Cease this act!"*

Shock burned deep and Cole immediately threw his globe across the room, breaking the Triad of Power. It lodged deep in the wood wall.

His attention shot to his love and every nerve stung at the sight; her pale face, her arms twisted around her torso as if for support, her legs pulled to her chest in a fetal position. Blood seeped from the corner of her bowtie lips and dainty ears.

He dropped to his knees and drew his fingers along her constricted body, afraid to touch her and cause more pain. Hot tears forced themselves past his eyelids. His heart cut into his throat.

Taravaughn raised an ethereal hand and the remaining crystal globes flew to opposite sides of the room. The air about him condensed to form a rocky mane, deep fire riding the waves of lava that wove through his stony hair. His fury filled Cole's heart. *"I will not permit such savagery. You have defiled that which is sacred. No Meridian shall cause my child's death without promise of rebirth."*

Cole's sorrow punctuated every word. "Taravaughn, please, deliver her. I know not how to rectify this wrong." He gazed at the closed eyes of his eternal companion. "My love," he cried, "my soul for thine."

Taravaughn's teeth flashed indignation. *"Gryffin, I demand justice!"*

James and Vincent stood silent. Cole's hair clung to his tear-streaked face like webs of containment. Taravaughn had every right to call upon Gryffin for justice. Every part of Cole's grieving soul wanted the great God of Conformance to end him with a single strike of his sharp beak. No price he paid would be enough for what he'd done to Mianna's soul.

Lowering his head, his whisper fell to Mianna's bosom. "Just save her, I pray thee."

Thick ambrosia waves undulated through the room and in a swift sweep rose. Long ivory robes flowed and then settled to adorn the Goddess of Love from the band of silver above her breasts. Trails of golden hair fell past her hips to her knees. Feathers adorned her shoulders and upper arms, every one as supple as the sheer silk that clothed her. Her dark blue gaze lowered to Cole.

A voice as melodic as love itself sent cherishment through his soul. *"He is not alone in his offense. Ancient devotion placed cause in this state. I call upon mercy, Gryffin. Withhold thy judgment for a time. The gift of love may offer salvation. Allow the rest of her natural life before vengeance is decreed."*

Taravaughn lifted his square chin and peered at him. His nostrils flared.

A shrieking cry pierced the warmth of Arylin's succor and Cole gazed around the room, watching for Gryffin to join the others in their spiritual presence. Linda followed his action, though he knew she'd see nothing aside from their solemn countenances and the destruction the harsh wind caused. His quick scan revealed that Elaina had fainted and Vincent had covered her with the discarded comforter.

Vincent glanced at her without moving his head and then looked back at Cole. He was sure Kid's emotions were on high volume at that moment.

Light shifted, morphed into beams directed toward the east wall. Shadows gathered, thickening to form the depths of an outlined spirit. Eight-foot wings spanned from an arched back and curled to accommodate the width of the room. The head of an eagle rose until the tall crown of feathers tipped the ceiling. Severity flashed in Gryffin's deep-set eyes as he lowered his gaze to Anna and then swept it to Cole.

Cole bowed his head as shame caused his breath to hitch.

Gryffin's voice penetrated his soul. *"Actions with eternal consequence must face verdict. Love's gift of one heart remains in the balance and will determine judgment. You are to serve her for the rest of her soul's life."*

Chapter Twenty-Four

Vincent's thoughts battled with his emotions as he neared his master bedroom. Elaina had promised to keep their abilities a secret when she learned he could manipulate the elements...before the promise band.

A magic man has cast a spell on me and I'll be that wizard's wife, whatever it takes.

The words sent a cringe up his neck. Though innocent, the disclosure hurt. He set his hand on the door handle and opened the latch. *Temper this. Understand.*

Elaina glanced at him from the edge of the bed as he entered, her brilliant blue eyes dull. Puffy lids held soaked lashes, tears pooling around the edges and falling to her freckled cheeks.

His heart clenched. He held out his hand, but she blinked away her gaze. "Take my hand, Elaina. We need to talk."

Gingerly setting her fingers in his palm, she choked out her words. "Don't leave me, Vince. I couldn't take it...if you left me."

What? How could she ever believe it would come to that? He watched as her shoulders jerk with stifled sobs. It crushed his soul.

The mattress dipped as he sat at her side. "I love you, Elaina. I'm not going to leave you. We can work through anything."

Elaina's lips quivered. "I didn't mean to tell Linda. I didn't mean to even imply you were wizards." She wiped a cheek dry and more tears spilled to replace them. "And when Cole sent us to the parlor after she threatened to go to see Lord Dressen..."

"I know Linda badgered you, Elaina. Cole told me you tried to avoid the topic."

"But, Vince," she turned to him, her eyes widening as she spoke. "That's not all."

Vincent's brows pulled together at the frantic plea in her tone. What had happened to rob her of her spirit? Confidence had always shown strong in her gentle ways. The woman before him sounded...broken.

"She figured out much more." Words tumbled forth in a rush and guilt heated Vincent's skin. All the changes, the secrets...she had needed someone to talk to. He should have been there, supported her as she came to terms with her new life. He watched as her brows rose with her exclamations.

"When she sat in the chair across from the hearth, she asked who the man was in the portrait. I told her it was Sylis Shilo, your father. When she looked at me the way she did, I knew I'd said the wrong thing. She asked how the founder of the city could be your father and if he was than you had to be centuries old. And how could you live that long unless you were a wizard."

Her shoulders drooped and she cocked her head. "Vince, I knew it was you when the manor shook. It happened right after I had the conversation about being a wizard's wife with Linda. You blew up the study, didn't you? Your father's study."

A sigh blew through his nostrils. "James fixed it. Only a few old items were broken beyond repair."

"But it happened. You were so angry at me that you destroyed the room dedicated to your family's heritage."

He brushed his palm along her strawberry curls. "It was a misunderstanding and I over-reacted. Forget the study."

She wiped her cheek again. "And I didn't mean to—faint when everything happened."

Laughter puffed from Vincent's lungs. *So much worry about doing the right thing. Gods, I've been too shortsighted.* "And don't worry about fainting during the unbinding. It was traumatic."

"And it failed. Poor Anna. What's going to happen to her? To Cole?"

Through all of this, she's thinking about someone else? What was he thinking? Of course she was. This was Elaina.

His soul grasped the gift of having her in his life anew. "You're really something, you know that? You've entered a new world, taken on heavy covenants, dealt with this crazy family almost all on your own the last few days and you're worried about two people you hardly know."

A weak smile curved her lips.

"Well," he sighed, "James restored her health. Linda was making her comfortable in a new room last I saw. The gods charged Cole to serve her for the rest of her soul's life. If I know him at all, she'll be his only thought from here on out. She'll be happy."

Elaina lowered her gaze. "And Linda?"

He took a deep breath. "By rights, Cole could call for a partial memory recall. James is talking to her, seeing if she'll accept a promising. He's against tampering with her memory. In all honesty, it causes more harm than good." He looked back at his love. "Regardless, she needs to stay here until she takes part in the Chalice ceremony."

Vincent stroked a finger down her lips and then lightly kissed them. "Elaina, your life is changing fast. I'm sorry I haven't been there when you needed me. I promise to do better. All of this will take getting used to. Be patient with yourself. With us. Our love is stronger than the obstacles this union will throw at us."

Tears filled her eyes again and she set her hand along his jaw. "I love you, Vince. With all my heart."

Combing his fingers through her long curls, he cupped the back of her head with his palm. "I love you. More than you may ever know. And I can't wait to kneel beside the alter with you as my bride."

A wide smile lit her face and sparkles returned to her blue eyes.

He pulled her into a tender kiss. Elaina, his heart and soul. Nothing would keep him from loving her.

James leaned against the door jam as Linda tucked clean linens around Anna. She brushed her friend's pale cheek. He tilted his head, watching the compassionate gestures.

A thick sigh issued from her full lips and she leaned her elbows on her knees. As she lowered her brow to her palms, he quietly stepped to her side and placed his hand on her shoulder.

Meeting his gaze, the corners of her eyes dipped. Shame flashed in her blue irises.

"She's resting now," he whispered. "Why don't we go relax in the parlor? I'd like to talk with you."

Her chin quivered as a smile teetered into place. She nodded.

Jittery steps punctuated her walk. As they passed the banister sentinel, she wavered and her hand lifted to her brow.

"It's okay, Leenja." In a swift dip, James scooped her into his arms.

She wrapped her arm around his neck and her head rested near his collar. Waving his finger at the door, it opened and he eased over the threshold. He slowed as they approached the sofa but she showed no desire to be released.

"The cushions are probably more comfortable."

She peeked at him through the top of her lashes. She blushed and looked at the large leather seating. "Sorry." She let go of his neck. "I...just..." Shoveling her hair behind her ear, she motioned to the couch. "Yeah, I mean... The sofa's fine. Any where's fine."

James lowered her onto the soft pillows and then pulled an ottoman before her. Taking a seat, he leaned his elbows on his knees.

She quickly swung her legs over the edge and pushed herself to an upright position. Raking her fingers through her hair, she blinked at him with a crooked smile. "Thank you."

"My pleasure."

"Um," she patted her thighs. "You really didn't have to carry me in here."

"No trouble at all." He furled his brow. "I'd offer you a drink after everything that happened, but I think it might not be the best idea with the spell you received."

Linda glanced at the bar and then blinked her gaze back to him. "Oh, yeah. Um, what was that Cole did to me?"

James lowered his gaze, but kept a small grin. "That was a calming draught. Nothing more."

She nodded and looked away. "It sure felt like more."

"Your heart was searching for reprieve." He leaned his head with a sympathetic gaze. "Leenja."

Her gaze snapped to him and he started at the quick response. He furled his brow. "Did I say something wrong?"

"My name." She flopped her hand. "Would you say that again?"

"Leenja?"

A breath of laughter puffed from her lips. "Wow," she breathed. "I love that."

James smiled. How could she draw his attention away from his concerns so easily? He watched her, eager to know what he had done this time. "What do you love?"

"How you say it. Your unusual accent. My name is Linda and you pronounce it *Leenja*."

A chuckle rumbled in his chest. That's it? Such a simple thing? What a pleasure. Pressing his lips together, he nodded. "I'm glad you like it."

A sparkle danced in her eyes.

"Leenja," he grinned as she tried to hide her smile. "I heard your prayer to Gryffin as we formed in the park." He took her hands in his. "And I know what happened with your husband."

Her cheeks lost their color and her smile faded. She gnawed at her lower lip, blinked several times.

James tightened his grip.

As she looked toward the far side of the room, moisture coated her eyes. She swallowed hard, but didn't stifle the hiccup. "I can't blame him...for going to her. Look at me. But my girls—I can't live without my girls."

As if the words slapped him in his face, James flinched. *What? Of all the unbelievable things she could have said, she said that?* His voice rose with his shock before he could harness it. "What do you mean you can't blame him for going to another woman? And what about how you look? You're beautiful."

Confusion jotted his thoughts. He shuffled in his seat and his hands fumbled over hers. Shooting to a stand, he launched into a stride around the chairs. He halted in front of the hearth, ran his hand over his chest. His cheek quirked and he glanced back at her.

"I'm sorry," she choked. "I didn't mean to bother you. Especially with all that happened and you being so nice to me."

He shook his head and held out his hand to emphasize his view of her. "Leenja, you are a beautiful, voluptuous woman. How can you think..." he turned to the hearth. Had he just called her voluptuous out loud? Heat rose to his face.

"Um..."

James looked back at her as she blinked her gaze to her hands and then she quickly withdrew a cigarette from her pocket. As she lit the end, she glanced in his direction. "You said I shouldn't have a drink, but I need something."

He grinned and returned to the ottoman, reclaiming his seat. Lifting his finger, he circled the tip of her cigarette. A tiny conduit appeared and the smoke trailed into the void.

She looked at him, eyes wide.

"I rarely smoke. The night air can have the remains."

"You're amazing."

His grin widened, pressing dimples into his cheeks. "So, you think I'm better looking than Vincent, you love how I say your name, *and* you think I'm amazing. I guess I'm doing something right."

Full lips pinched into a quirked smile.

Rounding back to the reason he needed to speak with her, he cupped her hand in his. "I must ask you, Leenja, to remain at the manor. I know you agreed to a short stay but under the circumstances it's imperative to ensure silence. What has taken place must never be spoken of outside these walls."

Linda flushed, her smile slid into a slight frown, and then her blonde brows rose. "James, you have my word. I'll never speak of this to anyone."

"Would you be willing to accept a promising?" He reached into his pocket and withdrew a champagne diamond wristlet. "It's a promise band. Once placed on your wrist, the promises you make upon acceptance are difficult to be broken."

"I'll do anything to prove how deeply sorry I am for what I tried to do."

He slid the adornment over her hand and gazed into her eyes. "Promise me you will honor our privacy."

"I promise."

"Promise me what happens within our family will remain silent."

"I promise."

"Promise me our nature and our ways will not be shared."

"I promise."

"That will do."

She shook her head and her voice held a tremor as she spoke. "And James, I promise to never try to use your wizardry for gain."

Smiling, he lightly kissed the promise bracelet. It morphed, molding to the curves of her wrist. He brushed his fingers across her cheek. "I wish I could ask for more promises from you. But I believe that would be inappropriate."

Linda's lips pinched into a sassy smile and he knew she wished he would go ahead and at least hint at those promises.

Chapter Twenty-Five

Cole dragged the towel down his face and then smoothed it over his wet hair. Exhaustion racked his body, despite the long shower. He sighed and smeared the steam from the mirror to catch his distorted reflection. His onyx eyes stared back at him, filling the hollow of his heart with guilt.

The rest of her soul's life. The unbinding failed. When she dies, so does her... His Adam's apple bobbed and he turned from the mirror to avoid the sight. He supposed he should be grateful for the chance of serving her that long. He grabbed a towel and wrapped it around his torso. Stepping into his room, he peered at the old clock on his dresser. Time. There wouldn't be enough.

Raking his fingers through his damp strands, he took a deep breath to steady himself. He'd begin today, making her life everything it could be. Anything she desired would be his pleasure to fulfill. She was an artist now. He'd have a studio fashioned. Every tool imaginable would be available.

Her apartment was papered in yellow. Daffodils, forsythia, roses... He scratched his chin. What other flowers were yellow? Whatever they were, he'd have the topiary sculpted with them. A smile crept onto his lips. At least he knew she liked roses.

Shedding the towel, he grabbed his robe and tied the belt tight. His fingers bunched into a fist as he swung open the door and marched into the hall. He'd fill her room with all the yellow roses he could find in the gardens. That would be a good start.

His newfound enthusiasm revitalized his steps and for the first time in centuries, true happiness filled his heart. The sense of beginning anew colored his outlook with possibilities of the present. He had Anna's life ahead of him and time be damned, he'd revel in every moment. She was his, and she knew despite all the displacing developments, he was hers. Whatever lay beyond the present could wait.

A door opened to the left and he halted with a step. "Anna."

A hint of insecurity played on her lips as she held to the latch.

"I thought you were resting. Do you need something?"

"You were gone and...I can't stop thinking. I lay in bed and all these memories kept running through my head." Placing a hand on her chest, she twisted her gown strap around her finger. "They make me hurt...inside. Nothing makes sense. I looked...and you weren't here. So..."

Compassion swelled in Cole's heart and etched across his brow. All her memories had been restored; her motherless childhood, daily uncertainty of shelter or food, loss of the one parent who struggled as a street sweep to provide what little they had. Then, receiving free will—a gift granted at birth but stolen, ordered by a man who'd pursued her and ultimately abused his power to have her. From bliss to pain and then left without a soul's ability to comprehend it all. How he wished he could relieve her ache.

He stepped inside and brushed his fingertips across her temple. "I'm so sorry. I wasn't there but I'll always be near."

Her arms wrapped around his waist, she bunched his robe into her fists. She laid her head on his chest and he rested his cheek on her dark hair, stroking the soft locks. With a sigh, Anna cuddled closer.

He longed to know exactly what she was feeling. With James' potion still in effect, he felt crippled. "Everything is okay, now," he whispered.

Anna tilted her head back, peering at him with the most beautiful blue eyes he'd seen. The call of her love echoed deep in his soul, just as it had in the alley, the shower, the time he'd comforted her after Kid's tantrum, and during her plea before the attempted unbinding. Truth drove understanding deep and he comprehended eternal union anew.

Framing her face with his hands, Cole gazed at the cherubic face of his love; every curve of her bow-tie lips, each lash that made up the thick fringes on her lids, the gentle slope that led to the rounded crown of her nose. His words flowed from his tongue, thick with affection. "How I love you."

"And I you," she breathed. "Promise me forever."

"Forever and always." The whisper sent licorice and cream, the musk of love's promise.

Her tongue met his, a silky feather rounding its tip. He relished the sweetness, losing himself in each gentle caress. His breath became hers. Anna's grip tightened as she gasped and rose to her toes, inhaling the Breath of Zephyr as if it held her life.

Fanning his fingers, he braced her as the gift intensified. She'd endured five long lifetimes of searching, waiting to taste the scent of his love and he would let nothing break the bond until she was ready to let go.

Delectation coursed through Cole's veins as his sensual gift fed her need. His head hummed, palms and soles tingled. He drew tiny circles on her temple until a gentle pull led him further into the room. No hesitance entered his mind. No warning of harm battled with his heart. Only the blessed consent from the gods filled his soul and he welcomed the moment unrestrained. He rolled his shoulder, sending a command to the door. It swung closed with a soft *click.*

Light peeked into the shadowy room from the vanity. The wide dresser mirror reflected the glow, bathing them in its wake.

Anna slowly released the kiss. Unable to abandon the pleasure, Cole traced the curve of her mouth, its gentle arc, delicate slope. Her head tilted back and a soft sound rode her sigh as he trailed kisses along her jaw to the supple skin beneath her ear.

The song of morning birds drifted from a distance. The clamber of tunes wove together until a distinct chorus emerged. Cole's senses heightened as he recognized the melody. The Song of Meridian filled his soul. Had James summoned the fowl in honor of a fortunate outcome? Surely, not. A gift from Arylin? Most likely, considering her call for mercy in light of ancient devotion. He awed at the Goddess of Love's grace.

Allowing the music to fill him, he moved with the instinct of his soul. He stepped wide, leading Anna into the most seductive dance known to the realms. Pulses flowed from his heart to hers as he relayed impressions of movement.

Across the floor of her guestroom, their steps echoed a measure. A spin turned as a pressing trill and Anna's breath hitched as Cole halted and pulled her back against his chest. Flattening his palms to her hips, he grazed them across her lower abs, over her apex, and to her thighs. His lips trailed her shoulder, nudging her gown's strap to the side. It fell to her arm.

Cole's hands dropped to his side. Stepping back, he paced around Anna to stand before her. She watched him, breasts heaving, fists bunched. The twelve inches that separated them seemed like miles, but he held his position, gazing deeply into her eyes, her soul. He could swear he saw the dance continuing in her wide pupils.

Anna slowly lifted her shoulder and the remaining strap dropped from its stay. The gown whispered to the floor. His robe tie loosened as she parted the panels and then trailed her palms up his abdomen. Slipping them under his arms, they traveled his torso to his shoulder blades. Her nails grazed his skin with a downward stroke.

Thrill charged Cole's senses. A growl rumbled low in his throat. Her lips traced the planes of his chest and fire erupted in his core.

He pulled her into an embrace, palms relishing the dip of her waist, the curves of her hips. His muscles quaked with need. Greed overtook finesse and he grasped her thighs, lifting her to straddle his waist. Hot breath fell to his neck as she clung to him. The sensations nearly blinded him. He clenched his jaw and his plea came forth as a raspy whisper. "Anna..."

Her fingers tangled into his long hair and her husky voice rounded his ear. "My heart. My soul. My always, make love to me."

Salvation sang at her bid and he reached the bed in three long strides. Her hooded gaze swept down his torso as he laid her on the downy comforter. Leaning onto his elbows, he looked at the angel beneath him. As much as he wanted to join with her, her pleasure had to come first. If he had to tantalize every part of her, he would force himself into submission.

A quick breath punched from her lungs and she flung her arms around his neck. Desperation tinted her tone. "What's taking you so long?"

Her legs tightened around him, hips rose to meet him. Taking her lips with his, he united with the woman who owned his soul. Delirious rapture coiled with each heated caress. Withholding completion edged unbearable.

For Anna. His mind willed to prolong but his body barely obeyed.

Pleasure rode each breath as Anna closed her eyes and pressed her head into the mattress. Her fingers grazed his back and then met.

Anticipation drove Cole to the brink as he recognized the sign of the triad. His skin sizzled. Adrenaline pumped through his veins. Fire blazed in his groin, fighting against containment.

She inhaled a sharp breath. *"Unsigh, Colhart!"*

Energy flew through him like a bolt from past ages, sharing Anna's passion, joining it with his own. Cole exploded. Triumph consumed him. Waves of rapture shot through his core, legs, arms. With every surge, he sent his love through the enchanted gift given long ago; every dream of her, every touch he'd savored, every moment of joy they had shared, he sent to her heart. *"All my love."*

The years he'd searched and failed dissolved.

The grip on his back tightened and then slowly loosened. Her hands slid down his side to the blanket. Her stare wavered and then settled on the air over his shoulder. Her mouth fell slack and then her head lulled to the side.

A chill washed over him. "Anna?"

He brushed the hair from her face, framing it so her unfocused gaze would meet his. "Anna?"

His throat clenched. He brushed his fingers down her neck to feel her heavy pulse. Then lowering his gaze, his hand followed to rest over her bosom. No lift. No sigh.

"Anna, breathe! You have to breathe."

Regret littered his confusion. He'd never expected their joining to cause her distress, not after the gods had allowed their love. Bracing her jaw, he pressed his lips to hers. The Breath of Zephyr filled her's lungs.

Anna gasped and a quick quake shook her body. A wail ripped from her lungs. Cole scooped her into his arms and held her tight as cries punctuated her short pants.

"Oh, my love. I never meant to hurt you."

Her trembling arms wrapped around him and she buried her face in his chest. "Oh, Sweet Arylin."

He rested his cheek on her tousled hair. "I'll find a way and nullify the spell."

"Huh?"

"I'll see to it this never happens again."

She peeked up at him from the tops of her lashes. "Wait. What?" She gasped a quick breath and released it unceremoniously. "Cole, that was the most amazing experience of my life. It better happen again."

The frank statement held a touch of humor and Cole furrowed his brow. "What?"

"Although," she held up her finger, swallowing with the little dip of her head. "If Father knew exactly what we did, he'd be irate, married or not."

"Father?"

"I can hear him right now." She lowered her chin and her tone mimicked a deeper voice. *"Mianna Newton, of all the fool things you've done. What about your heritage? Shilo is no place for a Newton. That young nudnik won't be able to protect you in that city of sin."*

Cole's mind reeled and he leaned back to study her face. He hadn't been called a nudnik since... "Nudnik?"

She laughed. "Oh, you know better than to take offence to Father's opinions."

Glorious gods of the celestial plane! "Mianna?"

She squelched her cheek and cocked her head. "Cole, are you okay? Did my phenomenal love making knock you into another world?"

A breath of awe passed his lips as the corners lifted into a hesitant grin.

Combing his hair back with her fingers, she leaned into him. "Come here. No husband of mine is going to make love to me and act like he's gone crackers."

She lay against his chest and then patted the place over his heart. Wrapping his arms around her, he held her tightly against the spot.

"Oh, Cole. I love you. I don't care if you are a wizard from another world." She peeked up at him. "With a funny name," she added with a snort.

"Colhart. Who ever heard of Colhart?" She closed her eyes, nuzzling his neck. "You're perfect. So perfect."

Mianna. Words couldn't express his feelings.

Warmth lighted on his soul and as if time warped, images of the Taravaughn's anger during the unbinding appeared before his inner eye. Arylin's words drifted through his mind.

"The gift of love may offer salvation."

The atmosphere thickened and recognizing the arrival of deity, Cole lifted his gaze. An ambrosia cloud billowed beside the bed and the Goddess of Love's spiritual presence took form within the soft halo. A gentle smile adorned her pink lips and love flowed from her dark blue eyes.

Reverence flooded Cole and he sent his thoughts in praise. *"Arylin, Goddess of Love."*

Her melodic voice spoke clearly to his soul. *"Do not offer your soul in praise, Colhart. I am not your creator."*

"You have returned my love to me. I feel I must praise thee."

Her blonde lashes swept down with her blink. *"I have not done so. You have carried it beyond the extents of this life."*

Cole searched her heavenly countenance, trying to understand. He had called Anna's soul beyond the boundaries of her lifetime?

Arylin watched as his thoughts raced, patience reflecting in her calm presence.

He'd created the charm for Mianna. Only her soul could control the spell, only she yielded the power to open the door so they could experience each other's joy. *Unsigh*—One heart. The joining of hearts and souls in shared passion. Dawning came in a rush.

Of course. The only spell created that allowed two souls' love to join as one. If they had joined...

He looked back at Arylin's kind gaze.

"Yes. The gift of one heart did call her soul to join yours. As you shared your memories of loving her, you carried her to a time free of the binding. If you hadn't shared this love, Colhart, if you had pursued your own satisfaction in its place, the binds would still hold."

Cole's heart thumped a wild rhythm. His throat tightened and tears seeped beneath his lids.

Arylin's gaze bore deep into his soul. *"But the transfer of temporal placement to a past life is not free of consequence. Advancement made over her last five life cycles has been lost. A crippling toll for a soul to pay. It will not be easy for my child."*

Cole stroked Mianna's hair. *"I will be here for her, Arylin. I will follow every rebirth and serve her for as long as my soul exists. This covenant I make with thee. She shall not be lost."*

"A covenant I accept only because your nature allows it and I know your heart."

A soft breeze filtered through the room, dispersing the divine connection.

Awe held Cole's gaze suspended. His mind whirled with the facts set before him. The truth seemed impossible to grasp while his arms refused to let go. They welded into a tight embrace.

Mianna.

"Um, Cole?" Mianna's muffled voice spoke against his shoulder. "I can't—breathe."

"Neither can I," he whispered.

She leaned her head to smash her nose against his jaw.

"Really. Cole, I can't breathe."

Realization loosened his grip but only by a slight margin. He shifted his gaze to look into her blue eyes.

"Say something. Something only you would say to me."

A smile crept up the corners of her mouth.

"Call me with thine eyes, my love.
May thy kiss be mine.
Fill my soul with Zephyr's breath.
Touch my heart alone."

Contentment washed across Cole's shoulders and down his arms. Muscles melted as the long forgotten language of his love lulled his heart. Mianna had been the only one to ever dilute him to the point of resembling a soggy rag and he basked in the pleasure.

"Bid the heavens part to we.
Send grace from above.
Arylin, Goddess of Love,
grant me now my prayer.
Sanction this, our unity
free from life's confines.
Love shall last 'or life's offing.
Promises of home."

Her warm breath pooled against his chest as she cuddled deeper into his embrace. "I love you, Cole."

He nuzzled her dark waves and filled his lungs with the scent of roses. "And I you, my love."

His fingertips drew circles on the nap of her neck and then traced the curves of her body with long strokes. He watched the gentle movement and wondered how Mianna would react when she realized she lived in a body born nearly four hundred years after she died. For that matter, what would she think when she found out she had died? And what of Anna? *No, it won't be easy.*

Soft hisses sounded as Mianna exhaled and he lightly brushed the hair from the side of her face. She looked like an angel sleeping in his arms. Eternity echoed through his soul and conviction burned bright. Whatever came their way, nature or man, he would be there for her. He had forever and nothing would change that again.

End Book One

Echoes

Cornerstone Deep Book 2

Chapter One

Exhaustion racked Cole's body. He squeezed his eyes shut and breathed deep to cleanse his lungs. The harm he'd caused Anna pulsed through his fatigued mind in fits of memory—distorted flashes that reminded him of the deceit, broken covenants, and ethereal anger. Pressing his palms onto his brow, his head sank deeper into the pillow. Did his actions really cost her soul five lifetimes?

He dragged his hand down his face and blew air through his pursed lips. He'd bound her soul and with his formidable skill with spells, he was unable to right his wrong.

The God of Life's fury rang in his ears as scenes of the night before haunted him. *"You have defiled that which is sacred. No Meridian shall cause my child's death without promise of rebirth. Gryffin, I demand justice!"*

His gaze turned to his love and he listened to the sweet sound of her steady breathing. Strands of sleep-messed hair fluttered along the pillow each time she exhaled. As God of Conformance, Gryffin had every right to end him when Taravaughn called for justice. Surely, that was the desired punishment. To sentence him to serve her for the rest of her soul's life only echoed Cole's intent from the start.

As the morning sun's light inched up the patchwork pattern of the comforter, he hitched his knee around her legs and formed his body to hers. How could he have imagined when he gave her the gift of *Unsigh* so long ago that the time would come when it would save her? In returning Anna's soul to a previous life it blessed them beyond his dreams. It freed the binding and... He buried his face in her long waves and the scent of roses filled him. He had Mianna back.

"Mianna." His whisper warmed his lips as it pooled against her neck.

She stirred and he pressed a kiss to her shoulder. "Cole." Her sleepy eyes fluttered open but closed as if her lids were too heavy. "Have you been awake long?"

He smiled as the sound of her voice dispelled his troubles. "A while. How are you feeling?"

She brushed his long hair with her fingers before resting it at her side. "So tired. I don't think I've ever been so tired." Her soft voice turned to a mumble. "You couldn't have given me a better wedding gift but," she drew a deep breath, "what did it do to me? What does Unsigh mean?"

Cole blinked his gaze to the side. *She doesn't know what Unsigh means?* He peered at her cherubic face. *Did she say wedding gift?* Realization flushed his senses. *The gift returned her memory to our wedding night. We truly are starting our life together over.*

He pulled the comforter up to her chin and wrapped his arm around her. "Unsigh means one heart, my love. It joins our passion when you create the symbol and utter the spell. It's an enchantment only you can call on."

"Oh," she breathed. "It's amazing...really. It's just...I'm so..."

As she drifted back into sleep, Cole's brow furrowed. Mianna's spell had never caused her fatigue, not even when her soul called upon it in Anna's lifetime.

A spray of sunrays pitched across his face as they hit the wide dresser mirror. With a scowl, he squinted at the glare and twitched his hand toward the window. The crepe sheers whipped closed followed by a thick *swish* from the burgundy drapes. The room plunged into darkness. Dim light from the vanity area competed with the beams' peek through the gaps around the window coverings. He heaved a sigh and sat up, resting his arm on his knee.

Perhaps it was everything she'd been through and she just needed rest. She'd experienced more trauma in the last week than he had in his sixteen hundred years. Her life as Anna hadn't been easy—abandonment, loss, and then manipulation by a man whose attention she'd refused. He raked his hand over his scalp. Then, to nearly lose her life while he tried to unbind her soul...

Cole gazed at the petite form beside him. He shook his head and brushed the dark hair from her face. How could Anna's features be so similar to Mianna's? The gentle slope of her nose, the curve of her bowtie lips. He tilted his head and gently stroked her cheek with his finger. Or was it love that colored his view? A smile bent his lips and he touched his brow to hers. No matter the reason. He had her back and he vowed to never lose her again.

A satisfied grin tugged at Lord Dressen's cheeks as he looked over the gathered noblemen. Their low voices filled the stately hall. Sunbeams poured through the twelve-foot windows, drowning the crowd in yellow haze.

With the majority of the Grand Marshals' court in attendance, the turnout met his expectations. His heavy brow furrowed and he lifted his chin. *Cole Shilo, you'll pay for taking Anna from me.*

The dull rumble of conversation subsided as he stepped to the Officiator's stand and took his chair at the center of the table. He nodded to the two gentlemen at the entrance and they stepped out, closing the doors behind them.

Lord Carrington tugged at his vest as he strode up the center aisle. His trusted friend moved with trained temperance, an admirable trait. Taking his place at Dressen's side, he leaned to him with a hushed voice. "Ninety-nine are in attendance. Lord Standish's men are the only ones not to sign in."

"We can do without them. What are twenty-two votes against ninety-nine?"

Carrington nodded and stroked his tailored beard. "One concern I feel I must voice, Kyle." His brown eyes twitched. "Standish may not hold the court's majority, but he's a strong believer in tradition. Tradition and religion go hand-in-hand. The men here control a vote, but many of their wives and family are faithful to the gods, including my own. They practice religious rites that encompass the Shilos as Sentinels. If this isn't handled with care, it could become nasty."

Dressen sighed as he glanced at the portraits of Senior Grand Marshals that lined the room. His gaze gravitated to the depiction of Sylis Shilo at the center of the hall. The Founder seemed to watch him, coal hair, onyx eyes, and square features set firm. Dressen sneered. *A wizard surrounded by noblemen.*

"Sentinels," he scoffed. "They're aliens. Nothing more. And their own laws protect us from their dimension's powers. What superior race agrees to such an arrangement? They're weak. Their kind has no place on Terra."

"Nevertheless, the faithful could rise up to protect them." Carrington looked at his cufflink as he straightened the gold piece. "And I'll be frank. Even though I see nothing wrong with how you achieved your goal with the girl, many will see it otherwise. Having the wizards bend her will as a servant was one thing, but calling for total compliance pushed the agreement's intention."

Dressen scowled. "The Wizards of Shilo Manor accepted my bid as any other. She broke the law and she was harvested. With the new curfew in play, she was no different from the homeless." He softened his tone. "It was the only way to get her past the idea that my standing separated us. Once she joined the household she admitted she wanted to be with me all along. She told me she loved me. Always had. She was happy."

He looked at his comrade and leered. "Cole Shilo's desire to have her took her from me." He pointed his finger to accentuate his view. "I know he has her up at that manor."

Lord Carrington cocked his head. "We have no jurisdiction within the Sentinel's home."

"You just deal with the charges."

"The only real proof we have is the vision you shared from that night she disappeared, Kyle. And that's another issue. You were only able to share it by way of the magical means Cole Shilo gifted you." His friend quirked his tan lips. "There's talk of a loss of integrity at the expense of..."

"A thief?" A growl rumbled in Dressen's throat as his blood seethed.

"A Sentinel, Kyle. You have to view this from these men's perspective. I know you're not religious, but religion is going to play a large part in what they decide."

"Then use their beliefs against them. Look into the covenants the wizards have made. Their long lives will show something. In eight hundred years, no man can live without error."

Carrington tugged at his collar as if it had suddenly become too small. "I'll make the assignment. But how do you expect to get to the girl if she's up there?"

A smile crept up Dressen's left cheek. "I'll find a way. You just call them in for questioning and I'll do the rest."

About the Author

Charlene A. Wilson is an author of tales that sweep you to other dimensions. She weaves magic, lasting love, and intrigue to immerse you into the lives of her characters.

She began writing in her early teens when her vivid dreams stayed with her long after she had them. The characters and worlds were so amazing, she brought them to life through her books.

She resides in a small community in Arkansas, USA, with her two beautiful daughters, husband, and a very chatty cockatiel named Todder.

Author site: http://CharleneAWilson.com
Facebook: http://bit.ly/CharleneAWilsonFan
Twitter: http://twitter.com/AuthorCAWilson

For media interviews, visit
http://charleneawilson.com/promotionals

Also by Charlene A. Wilson

Cornerstone Deep Series
The Transformation of Anna
Echoes
Destiny

One for Kami

Aumelan Series
Coming Soon!
Aumelan
World Beneath the Rock
Waters of Tiger Rod
Kingdom, Rise

Made in the USA
Charleston, SC
06 October 2013